WHAT DOESN'T KILL HER

WHERE SHOULD I START?
A Guide to The Disclosure Paradox *Series*

New to the series? *There are two entry points, depending on how you prefer to read.*

Option 1: Start with Book 3 (Character-First Readers)
What Doesn't Kill Her

Begin here if you prefer:
- Character-driven stories
- Psychological realism
- Government secrecy and survival narratives
- Minimal metaphysical framing

This novel stands alone and provides the emotional and ethical foundation for the entire series.

Option 2: Start with Book 1 (Discovery-Driven Readers)
The Disclosure Paradox

Begin here if you prefer:
- Suppressed knowledge
- Underground facilities
- UFO and nonhuman intelligence themes
- Team-based infiltration stories

Book 3 deepens the meaning of events in Book 1 but is not required to understand it.

Continue the Story with Book 2
The Disclosure Paradox: Salvation

This installment explores the ethical and existential stakes introduced earlier, asking what happens when ancient artifacts, modern science, and nonhuman agendas converge.

Reading Order Summary:
- **Chronological:** Book 3 → Book 1 → Book 2
- **Publication:** Book 1 → Book 2 → Book 3

Both are valid.

ADVANCE PRAISE FOR *WHAT DOESN'T KILL HER*

"Tangentially tethered to reality, the reader will find a complex tale of international violence and intrigue coupled with the application of psychic phenomena. Astute observers will identify many of the real people and places as the adventure unfolds."
—**John B. Alexander**, PhD

"Paul Vecchiet's third book, *What Doesn't Kill Her*, is an intriguing prequel that reveals how the book's hero, a seemingly average mom, perfects her psychokinetic powers to get even with government agents who must recruit her, or kill her. I was immediately taken in by the mysterious backstory and could not put it down until I found out how it ended!"
—**Steve Jacobson**, BSEE, retired aerospace engineer for NASA, Boeing, Northrop Grumman, and the US Navy

PRAISE FOR *THE DISCLOSURE PARADOX: SALVATION*

"... A gripping tale of international (and extraterrestrial) intrigue. The topics are as big as they get—the future of humanity, the Shroud of Turin, psychic phenomena, UFO lore—but the main characters, particularly Mary Ellen and Robert, help the author make the enormous ideas feel approachable and human-scaled. The book invites readers into complex debates but also works quite well as a conspiracy and SF narrative that's both thought-provoking and pulse-pounding. A tense thriller that deftly incorporates otherworldly elements."
—*Kirkus Reviews*

"*The Disclosure Paradox: Salvation* is indeed a roller-coaster ride of marvelous characterization, along with fast-paced action which grabs you and doesn't let go.... Prepare to be enthralled by aliens, UFOs, secret laboratories, psychic powers, the Vatican and the revelation of the Turin Shroud, which Paul weaves beautifully into an epic that will leave you wanting more. A wonderfully written book which deserves to be made into a film."
—**Philip Kinsella**, researcher and author of *The Eternal Avatar*

"Vecchiet weaves a plot of psychics and interdimensional aliens.... [he] opens the door to one possibility of where truth and myth, and spirituality and science may meet. If you're a fan of sci-fi, the paranormal, and the search for inner truth—sprinkled in with history and exotic locales—*The Disclosure Paradox: Salvation* should be on your reading list."
—**Tj O'Connor**, award-winning author of *The Whisper Legacy*

"Paul Vecchiet has made a blockbuster sequel to his sci-fi series *The Disclosure Paradox*.... *Salvation* is a fast-paced story...filled with exceptional details and plot twists, resulting in a 'can't put it down,' highly entertaining read which I strongly recommend."
—**David J. Keys**, PhD, author of *Discovering the Fullness of Reality: How Partial Truths Obscure the Union of Faith and Science*

PRAISE FOR *THE DISCLOSURE PARADOX, BOOK 1*

"A fascinating tale about a secret world that we only glimpse dimly through the eyes of a dedicated and obsessive group who give up everything to find the truth and stop a hideous plot to control our destiny. A beguiling blend of horror, science fiction, and riveting action, with realistic characters and plot twists that will leave you breathless. Highly recommended."

—**Frank E. Lee**, WXRT-FM, Chicago

"*The Disclosure Paradox* provocatively tackles some of life's heavy questions, especially regarding other life forms in the Universe. It was not long ago that unidentified anomalous phenomena were considered tin-foil-hat subjects. However, numerous government whistleblowers have come forward to admit that the phenomena really exist and are a threat to our national security."

—**Joseph Marino**, President, Shroud of Turin Education and Research Association, Editor, shroud.com

"Though presented in fictional form, anyone familiar with various anomalous phenomena will recognize the fact-based narratives depicted in *The Disclosure Paradox*. Thought-provoking. . . . The physical and spiritual are merged into Louis Silvani's life mission to understand a complex and rewarding destiny."

—**John B. Alexander**, PhD

"A wild ride! The characters are rich and believable. The ET subject matter is accurately portrayed. In the end Louis finds his roots, and I am left wondering what I can do to improve humanity!"

—**Steve Jacobson**, BSEE, retired aerospace engineer for NASA, Boeing, Northrop Grumman, and the US Navy

A DISCLOSURE PARADOX NOVEL
BOOK THREE

WHAT DOESN'T KILL HER

PAUL G VECCHIET

WRITE AWAY BOOKS
Carlsbad, California

Copyright © 2026 Paul G. Vecchiet. All rights reserved.

Published by Write Away Books, USA

Taking Authors From Idea to
Manuscript to Marketplace ™

writeawaybooks.com

PO Box 1681
Carlsbad, CA 92018

Print ISBN: 978-1-969838-01-9
ebook ISBN: 978-1-969838-11-8

No part of this book may be reproduced in any form or by any means without the express written permission of the author. Exceptions are made for brief excerpts used in published reviews.

Front cover design: Danny Hobart (www.dannyhobart.com), with concept by Paul G. Vecchiet

Cover portrait by Joao Paolo de Souza Oliviera on Unsplash (@joaoattitude1)

Additional cover photos by Dario Bronnimann (@dariobroe), Artur Stanulevich (@artstanulevich), Greg Johnson (@tornadogreg), and Michelle McEwen (@michellem18) on Unsplash

1

... HER FATHER'S BURDEN

Katrina filled the tub with cold water. She had learned to live through the sudden intrusions of pain only she could describe. It starts with being disoriented, then the symptoms get worse. An abrupt rise in body temperature signals a need for urgency. Her spine begins to burn and her head feels like it is being split in two down the middle, as if the hemispheres are repulsed by each other, forcing their way through her skull.

When she first experienced the sensations years ago, she was advised by a psychic assassin that cold water would slow down her neurotransmitters, giving her relief. Robert, her life partner, made it his responsibility to assist Katrina when he found out about her unique condition.

Robert rushed to the bathroom with a bucket of ice, dumping it into the tub. Katrina's condition made her hypersensitive to noise, and the crashing cubes and splashes compounded her misery. Robert helped her disrobe and guided her to the freezing water. She immersed herself gently. The ice-cold bath instantly soothed her. The burning in her spine and head pain subsided. Such was the routine she was destined to act out to alleviate this side effect of her psychic ability.

No longer hijacked by the pain, she asked Robert to bring her paper and a pen. Robert returned to her side, monitoring her for signs of hypothermia. Katrina proceeded to write a long-overdue letter to her only child, Emma.

Dearest Sweetheart,

I never thought I would live long enough to see you grow into the intelligent, lovely young woman you have become. I am so blessed.

You are the love of my life and always have been. You are the reason I survived the trials I was put through. You are the reason I rise in the morning.

I have often wondered what your young mind was thinking trying to process what was happening to me. Although you did not comprehend the dangers you were put in, I believe you sensed things were not the way they should have been.

I can't imagine any other family has ever endured the torture, the threats, and the betrayals that we shared together. I regret that I had to put Grandma through that. I wish I could have told her the things I am telling you. It's ironic. We weren't quite the nuclear family, yet we are the product of the nuclear age.

I prayed you would not be cursed with the gift I have. I am relieved to know that I did not pass that trait on to you. Every life-changing decision in my control was made with you in mind.

I am also relieved that you turned out to be "normal" emotionally. I know that you still have bad dreams about us being chased or seeing me suffer helplessly. I hope someday you find it in yourself to forgive me for not being like most normal mothers.

I will continue to love you dearly and look forward to seeing your smile again—hopefully, soon.

I will love you always,

Mom

With a sense of accomplishment, Katrina gave the pad of paper and pen back to Robert and exited the tub. Then she thanked him for his support, leaning her wet body against him, reaching up and pressing her cold lips on his. He didn't mind that she made his shirt and pants wet. Robert set the pad on the counter and reached for a towel, draping it over Katrina's shoulders, and pulled her closer while drying her back. She took the towel and finished drying herself as Robert left the room, taking her letter to Emma, still on the pad, with him.

Several minutes later, Robert knocked on the door. "Your dad is on the phone," he said.

Katrina's father was calling from a retirement home near Washington, DC. Now approaching ninety years old, Commander Edwin Juno Hermann, USN retired, knew his time on Earth was about to end. Katrina stopped what she was doing, stunned her estranged father would call. She had ended the relationship with her father after the passing of her mother.

Robert opened the door and handed Katrina the phone. She looked at it like she was looking at a strange object. The old man sat listening for something, a voice, breathing.

"Hello? Katrina are you there? It's your father."

Katrina continued to look at the device in her hand that relayed the voice she hadn't heard for years.

"Katrina!"

The shout startled her out of her trance-like condition. She raised the phone to speak. "I'm here Dad. I . . . had to put something I was working on down to pick up the phone. You probably should realize I am very surprised you called."

The old man didn't respond immediately. Katrina could hear him put his hand over the receiver to block a coughing episode. His voice was much weaker and more throaty than the thunderous and direct one she remembered.

"I won't take too much of your time, Katrina. Matter of fact, I am running out of time, but I didn't call about that so you would feel sorry for me." Her father paused for a breath. Katrina let him continue. "I need you to come to DC and see me. I . . . I am not proud of how we are—separated, not caring as a family should be."

Katrina resisted saying anything defensive or offensive, even if it was the truth. Hearing her father express his feelings, any feelings that resembled a human, was unexpected and strangely awkward.

Her father paused to wait for a response. His silence was rewarded by hearing her first words—which were not what he wanted to hear.

"For the record, we never really behaved like a family under your command. So, you're dying and you want to see me before it's too late?"

"I am ill, and I will probably not make it to the new year. But the reason is not what you think. There is something I need to tell you face-to-face, and there's something I have to show you so you have a better understanding of how we all got the way we are. I am not calling for my benefit, Katrina. I am calling for your benefit, your sanity, and your self-awareness."

"Alright Dad. You got me. I mean, damn. You know what I went through. If you are going to tell me something I didn't know about me, you, Mom, or my brother, I want to be there."

* * *

After saying she'd be there as soon as possible, Katrina set down the phone, thinking about their past. Katrina's father would mistreat and verbally abuse her mother, even as her mother succumbed to the deterioration of Alzheimer's. He was not a nurturing father. Although she understood that it was wrong in her own mind to take herself out of his life, she felt visits would resurrect unbearable memories of sorrow and pain. Katrina privately asserted that her father had made little effort to make her mother's last months more comfortable. Now that it was his turn to pass, she would not mistreat him as he had his wife. She imagined releasing a fury of words of scorn and revenge upon seeing him. Would it matter now? Would the fact that her father was facing *his* last days prompt him to apologize for the way he had treated his family?

As promised, Katrina booked the first available flight from Santa Fe to Dulles International Airport. Two days later, Robert drove her ninety minutes to Santa Fe to catch a midday flight to Dulles with a two-hour layover in Dallas. She arrived at Dulles International Airport after 9 p.m. Her bag seemed heavier than when she first boarded, as did her heart when she arrived. On the phone, her father had indicated no sign of reconciliation, and it troubled her. She picked up her rental car and drove to Alexandria where she found lodging near her father's retirement home.

While pacing the small hotel room, clicking aimlessly through the selections on her TV, she recalled being the unwilling witness to her father's insults. The soundtrack of her youth ran through her mind like scratchy vocals of an angry singer: the acts of her obedient, docile mother being berated by an obnoxious, boorish man, while

Katrina hid from his view. However, unlike popular sitcoms of that era, there was no laughing audience.

The next morning, Katrina was awakened by her father's call. Even in his late eighties, he still rose with the dawn, as if readying himself for reveille and falling-in call, maintaining the warrior mentality. Most of the people that lived in the retirement home were known by their first names. Edwin Hermann was known to everyone as Commander, wearing his hard-earned rank everywhere. The staff followed his demand to conciliate. Having never shed his rank, not even with his family, he commanded his daughter to pick him up at 10 a.m. He needed her to take him to Arlington National Cemetery to visit an "old friend."

Katrina arrived fifteen minutes early to find the commander, with the assistance of an orderly and a quad-cane, entering the lobby. Her plan to sit and warm up to him over a cup of coffee was quashed when her father insisted they leave immediately.

The drive to the national cemetery took only twenty minutes. As she navigated the Beltway and the exits to their destination, Katrina's father controlled the conversation.

"How are they treating you, Dad?"

"Keep your eyes on the road. The orderlies tell us there is an accident almost every morning on this mess they call an expressway."

Katrina repeated the question.

"You saw it didn't you?"

"Saw what?"

"Respect! Order! I've instilled those civilians with a degree of uniformity and protocol!" The elderly man struggled to get his words out as he cleared his throat. "It's a wonder that place was successful before I arrived."

"I wanted to ask you . . ."

"Your father may be old, but he hasn't lost his wits—not like your mother."

Katrina resisted saying anything in defense of her mother. She sought to avoid stress and conflict during this rare visit.

"They look up to me there. In fact, I even settle arguments between the residents. You know there are all kinds living in that building—just like the service. You have to know how to talk to people. You have to recognize the situation. The other day—well, last month—something on the TV caused a couple guys to get into a shouting match about whether or not it's right to kneel at a sports event during the national anthem!"

"There are a lot of people that claim it's disrespect for the flag."

"Is that what you think? My God! Where did you get that?"

"No, Dad!—I'm just saying, not everyone thinks like us!"

"Well, they are wrong! Not many things are important enough for me to stop a crossword puzzle and get out of my chair, but for this argument, I was not going to be idle." Katrina's father caught his breath before he resumed. "First, I said to the two, it is not a protest! Protests are vocal where people hold signs or banners. It's a demonstration. Second, their cause is not unreasonable. What do you want them to do? Riot? That doesn't work. March? There would probably be arrests. This is their way of telling us that their life, their challenges, their treatment are not the same as others. Then I told them I didn't wear the uniform so we would let people who believe minorities should not have the same rights as others get away with it."

Katrina noticed her father raise a hand to cheek to wipe a tear away.

"That quieted both of them, since I was the only one who ever wore a uniform. I told them that even though I don't see anything wrong with kneeling as a demonstration, I love our flag and our country. The act of kneeling during the anthem is the ultimate sign of a free society."

Katrina changed the subject. "Who are we going to visit, Dad? Were you in the Navy together?"

"You'll find out soon enough. You *might* say we worked together—briefly." He coughed through nearly every word he spoke.

It was Katrina's first visit to Arlington National Cemetery. Her father had been there several times, some for official duty as part of an honor guard during the Korean and Vietnam Wars. After exiting the sheltered underground parking, Katrina buttoned up her light jacket. Edwin welcomed the fresh air on his face, a pleasant contrast to the staleness of the retirement home. A spring landscape greeted visitors paying respect to the fallen. Blossoms graced the hallowed grounds to herald nature's renewal. Katrina was struck by the symbolism. Death was not the finality most people fear. She believed death allowed one's spirit to seek a new existence based on the life just lived. She wondered about her father's spiritual fate, based on the callousness of his words and actions toward his family. Why was it so difficult for him to show kindness? Was his military bearing driven so deeply into his core that it made the effort of being a gentle and caring father unfathomable?

Katrina seated her father in a wheelchair borrowed from the retirement home, allowing him the independence to move under his own power, but his aged body was tough for him to move, little more now than a feeble skeleton with crepe paper skin. Even his will was muted. Frustrated, the retired Navy officer ordered her to exit through the visitors' center to the west, still not revealing his destination. He knew exactly where to go; he had no need for the map Katrina had picked up at the information desk. He directed her north on Schley, then left on Custis, uphill to Section 30.

"You can stop now. We are here."

"Whose grave are you going to, Dad?"

The once robust Navy officer slowly raised his trembling arm, extended his bony index finger, and pointed to a large granite stone marker not far from the walk: "JAMES FORRESTAL."

Katrina's eyes elevated, as did her heart. "You were friends with Forrestal?" she asked, surprised.

"We weren't friends." He paused, short of breath. "I would not have done what I did without his direct involvement in my career." Her father paused again to catch his breath. "Katrina, everything that happened to you was because of him. If I had known long ago, before I had even met your mother, that my future children would suffer because of my career choice, I would have stayed where I was in the Army, instead of transferring to the Navy."

This was as close to an apology as Katrina had ever imagined getting from her father. His words were not about lost opportunities of love and tenderness; they seemed to be about something much deeper. She remained silent, keeping her eyes on the stone marker.

Her father pointed to a bench near the walk and told her to sit and learn about how her fate had been decided before she was born. "Katrina, before I leave this prison of a planet, I want to let you know how it all happened." He scanned the cemetery grounds. In the distance he could make out a small group of people and an honor guard that was laying to rest a draped coffin. His own final resting place would likely be near there. He raised his head and looked up at the cerulean sky. It was the sky or something from the sky that started all the chaos that would affect his family.

WHAT DOESN'T KILL HER

* * *

Army Private Edwin Hermann's first assignment was at Roswell Army Air Field. It was July 9, 1947. His outfit had just completed a thorough sweep of a rancher's property, thirty miles north of the installation. The rancher and the town's citizens had done a good job of picking out choice fragments and parts of an exotic craft that had crashed a couple days prior. Various government agencies were dispatched to the town to retrieve those fragments from the private citizens and take the materials into custody. It was a most unpleasant activity for both sides. Fortunately, for him, Hermann's battalion was not involved in the mass confiscation and incursions.

Not long after returning to his station, Hermann, along with other expendable privates, was dispatched to recover wreckage from yet another crash, approximately seventy-five miles northwest of Roswell. Rumors circulated that there were bodies to be recovered — dead and alive. The Army did not want a repeat of the Roswell scenario, whereby the crash site had been compromised by curious townsfolk and souvenir seekers. Army recovery teams were staged in a bomber hangar at Roswell Field. Vehicles included half-tracks, jeeps with generators, flat-bed tractor-trailers, emergency vehicles, and covered 2 ½ ton trucks. Hermann's platoon was briefed on the top-secret operation. The members were advised not to talk while in transit nor at the site.

A security team was deployed immediately. Under normal crash circumstances, a recovery team would be on site to assist investigators in the identification of the victims' remains or in tagging aircraft parts. This particular recovery was crude and needed to be expedited. The objective? Retrieval and restoration of the site before daylight. Nothing was to remain: not a trace of evidence. The first team of soldiers at the site found a debris field three-quarters of a mile long and three hundred yards wide, laid out in a north–south grid with pieces ranging in size from that of a nickel to a car door.

The convoy drove two hours up a gradual incline through the desert brush. They entered the crash site through the north entry control point manned by armed military policemen (MPs) joining the first teams. The armed MPs were actively turning away unauthorized civilians. In contrast to the event at Roswell, the Army arrived first and were well prepared. As instructed, the men left the trucks, and using flashlights, three platoons moved in unison, abreast, keeping three yards apart. NCOs monitored from behind to ensure that no one pocketed artifacts for themselves. Boots shuffled along the desert soil and brush illuminated by scores of handheld flashlights painstakingly searching for any debris.

Fresh off the truck, Hermann bent down to tie his boot as his comrades joined the search crew. Commotion on the other side of the truck drew his attention to a two-man unit carrying a litter with an olive-drab green blanket draped over a body. The men paused for a rest and gently placed the stretcher on the ground. The blanket, protecting the identity of the victim, slipped from its original position to reveal the head of a nonhuman creature. It turned to meet Hermann's gaze. The private's shock transformed into abject terror as his brain was flooded with words he didn't think up: *"Help me! Help me! I am dying. We are scientists, not combatants."*

Apparently sensing the private was not a threat, the alien directed everything left of his energy to impart his knowledge to the private, telepathically. This last act would ensure the alien's mission had not been a complete failure. Among the bits of data transferred was a visual of the crash and the sequence of events leading up to it.

The medics returned. Realizing the secret had been exposed, they quickly repositioned the blanket, carrying their charge away from the area and Hermann's sight. Hermann found himself standing by the truck, confused and uncertain about how long he had been there. As he turned around to head back to his platoon, he bumped into an Army major. "What are you doing here, Private . . . *Hermann*?" the officer asked, reading the soldier's name tag. "Did you see something unexpected?"

"Sir, I just stopped to tie my boot . . ."

"And you saw an alien. Not only did you see the alien, but something happened to you, didn't it? I was watching you."

Private Hermann was at a loss for words. He actually wasn't sure what had happened: He had been caught in a brief but fateful trance. That brief encounter would become the driving force behind everything that would happen to Hermann for the rest of his life.

From the moment the major approached and challenged the young private, Hermann's life took a direct detour away from the rudimentary and ordinary. The major was from Army Intelligence, in charge of the investigation of the wreckage and its technologies. To Private Hermann's surprise, the officer walked him back to his platoon leader and advised the lieutenant that he was requesting that

Hermann be transferred to the major's detachment with the Signal Corps, immediately. The company commander was then advised that a letter of transfer would be on the captain's desk promptly, with official orders from Headquarters, US Army Security Agency, Fort Meade, Maryland.

The major led Hermann back to the site commander's tent for an interrogation. "Sit down, private," he commanded.

"Am I in trouble, sir?"

"Only if you want to be. You tell me the truth, and there is no problem. Tell me everything you can about what happened back there."

"Everything, sir?"

"As much as you can remember. Don't omit any details."

The frightened private looked down at the ground clasping and rubbing his hands.

"When I got off the truck, I noticed laces untied on my boot. I walked to a trailer and as I was tying the laces, I looked toward the other side of the trailer and saw a stretcher with a blanket. The blanket slid off and that's when I saw it."

"Describe what you saw."

"The large smooth head—gray-green, large black eyes—no eyelids, looking directly at me. I couldn't look away. I don't know if I even tried, sir."

The major took out a cigarette, lit it, and resumed speaking with the first puff. "You were in the same position, locked on it for a long time. What was happening as you were in that trance?"

"I heard its words in my mind asking for help. It was dying. They were scientists." Hermann looked up from the ground for the first time to look at the major. "Scientists." He repeated with the look of someone who had too many questions.

"There's more," Hermann continued. He became more assertive as he rose from the chair, the light above casting his shadow directly on the major.

"I saw the inside of their craft. I saw the crew. They all had their hands on a console that they stood behind, side by side—five creatures. Each one linked to the craft through their mind. They navigated and operated with their minds. They were searching for the craft that went down at Roswell a couple days ago. Their craft is not like our flying machines—it's like its own organism. They got within range of a radar test at White Sands and it breached the hull

... HER FATHER'S BURDEN

of the ship. The shock made the creatures lose physical and mental contact with the craft. Out of control, it crashed."

Private Hermann stopped talking. He blinked, noticing his brash position in relation to the major whose complete attention was focused on him.

"Excuse me sir . . . I . . ." Hermann looked back and rushed to his chair.

The major was silent trying to understand what just happened. He put out his cigarette and adjusted himself on the metal chair.

"Is that the only information you received from the alien, Private Hermann?"

"Sir?"

"Do you have any more information beyond what you told me about the craft?"

"The craft?"

"Can you repeat what you just told me, Private?"

"Did I tell you something?"

The major realized Hermann had been in another trance as he detailed how the craft worked and why it crashed. Hermann would not be able to recall the information again.

"You just described to me how and why the craft crashed. You gave details on how the creatures use their minds to navigate."

Hermann's eyes widened.

"I think that the alien transmitted information to your brain that you are not aware of. Ten minutes is a lot of time for thought to be transferred. There may come a time when that information comes to you again. When it does, I want you to be under my command. What I am about to tell you is top secret, not to be uttered again."

The private's face showed concern as the major explained his mission.

"Private, as Intelligence Officer, I received a scrambled radio message today from the Office of the Secretary of the Navy that I was to collect as much information, material, parts, equipment, even bodies as I could. I have been directed to get teams to pack the items securely and ship them to a lab at Wright Field in Dayton, Ohio. At Wright Field, the items will be unpacked and identified for further research. I have been advised there are plans in motion for a secret cadre of high-ranking leaders and scientists to be established to manage information and set policy for these kinds of incidents."

Private Hermann remained motionless and completely transfixed on every word from the major. "Private, you are going to be my assistant. That means you and I will fly to Dayton to manage the identification process."

Young and impressionable, Private Hermann was overwhelmed with this new information and with the drastic change in direction of his military career. Hermann's head was full of questions demanding answers, but he was not comfortable asking them yet.

"Private, this job you will have is important," the major said. "I need you to think about and to be sure you comprehend what is expected of you. I realize this is a lot to process in such a short time. For some reason, you stumbled upon that alien. For other reasons, that alien made contact with your mind. You are probably in possession of highly sensitive information that, if intercepted by any foreign agency, would be a threat to our national security. I have to handle you as if you are carrying top-secret plans. Until we go to Wright Field, I am placing you on leave."

"Sir, I don't have much leave saved up."

"You will not be charged for leave. You will be in quarters at Roswell but not in the barracks. You will move your things to the Signal Corps building where I have my office and residence. That will be your new home. This will also minimize your exposure to others, and let you have some time to think about what lies ahead."

The private took little time in making the move. At Roswell, his new sleeping quarters were much improved. He shared the latrine with the major, had more personal space, and had his own desk and a window.

Later that week, Private Hermann accompanied the major on a flight to Wright Field to meet scientists assigned to the Technical Data Laboratory. The scientists escorted the major and Private Hermann to a large hangar in Area B where the wreckage was being inspected, cataloged, and either reassembled or packed for shipment to labs around the country. The cavernous interior of the hangar provided an expansive setting for witnessing the craft's pieces under inspection by teams of white-smocked scientists and engineers. Private Hermann stepped into what he normally would have considered to be a fantasy world. Hermann was in awe as he marveled at the activity. He didn't notice the man in the tailored suit and fedora hat approaching his major.

"Major, I am delighted you were able to come in such short notice. And this must be Private Edwin Juno Hermann!"

The private was startled to hear his full name from the stranger, and he remained silent, glancing at his major.

"Private Hermann, meet James Forrestal, Secretary of the Navy." Hermann could not find words beyond, "Hello, sir."

Mr. Forrestal held out his hand. Absorbed in the wonder of the moment, the private was late in recognizing it and rushed an awkward shake. Forrestal, the private, and the major walked around the work area, careful not to interfere with the scientist crews immersed in their contact with exceptionally exotic material and equipment. Secretary Forrestal allowed the major and private better access to the extremely sensitive activity. Private Hermann was silent while Forrestal and the major discussed the high technology sitting in plain sight. As the three strolled the scene of technology triage, Hermann recognized the random parts on the tables and floor. Forrestal and the major continued to walk while the private was moved to stop and inspect one specific part, being cued by a "feeling." The Secretary of the Navy and the major looked back to notice the private in deep conversation with a growing number of attentive researchers. The men and women in the white smocks began taking notes, amazed by the private's technical acumen. Forrestal and the major returned to the throng, warranting everyone's attention, especially that of Private Hermann. They asked him to walk with them, much to the disappointment of the team of scientists. The major explained that the scientists' tasks involved sorting, categorizing, and tagging. The private's work would commence after the sorting was complete.

At the end of the walk, Forrestal ushered the major and the private to a room adjacent to the high bay hangar. During the war, it served as a briefing room for student pilots of the bombers used for training. Except for a few file cabinets, a watercooler, a 55-gallon drum trash can, a steel top table, and four chairs, the room was vacant.

Forrestal motioned to the table. "Let's sit down, Private." Hermann and the major did as Forrestal directed. Forrestal and Hermann were adjacent to each other sharing a corner. The major sat across from Forrestal. "You have a very important role, Private. Prior to coming here, I was instructed to explain to you your newly assigned position. For security reasons, I don't have anything in writing, so you must listen. Please ask for clarification if you don't understand anything I will be talking about. Mind you, there are decisions still being made about how the government is going to manage information collected by crashes or sightings,"

The private sat still, erect, with his hands placed symmetrically on his parallel legs, shoes parallel, and close together. His mouth was closed, eyes, wide open—exemplary military bearing.

The major also sat attentive and did not take out his Lucky Strikes, respecting Forrestal who did not smoke.

"Private Hermann, last June 24, a civilian pilot flying over the Cascades in Washington State observed nine flying discs in formation, flying at a very high rate of speed. Now, this is not the first sighting of such objects, but it was the first to gain widespread attention by the newspapers. Prior to the crash a few days ago, there were over one hundred reports of similar sightings. Many of those reports came from credible, high-ranking soldiers and reputable civilians. All branches of our defense investigated. We know as much about this type of activity as we did before it happened. In addition, the appearance of articles in papers have caused people to be fearful, losing trust in us. For these reasons, President Truman is putting together plans to set policy on the release of information and the collection of debris and possible life forms."

"Still no official word, sir?" the major asked.

"Nothing yet, Major. This kind of Executive Order takes time. The President's first order of business is national security. He wants to safeguard information gained by these crashes from the Russians. He wants to keep a tight lid on the news from these crashes and sightings from now on. The public doesn't need to know about every report. Major, I think you succeeded in calming the situation by having your teams debrief witnesses at Roswell. You may have noticed that news reports indicated the object was a misguided weather research balloon. That is an example of how the President wants to release news about such incidents."

Forrestal got up and served himself water from the cooler in a paper cup. Taking sips, he remained standing.

"Private, the major told me what happened to you at the Corona debris field. From what I saw minutes ago, his belief that you have been given technical data on the craft by a dying alien seems accurate. How do you feel, having this ability? Do you have any concerns about what we need you to do?"

"Sir, um... Mr. Secretary. I have had a couple days to think about what happened. Actually, sir, I feel... very different from before I saw the alien. I don't know how to describe it. I feel like myself, but I am thinking older—no not older, confident. For example, it feels more natural talking to you, even though I am only a private and you . . . you're the Secretary of the United States Navy! Does that answer your question, Mr. Secretary?"

The major interjected, "Private, are you saying that the alien not only gave you technical information, but it gave you an ability to communicate and maybe even lead confidently?"

"I think so, sir. I used to stumble on my words. Or I wouldn't be able to explain what I was thinking. I don't feel that way anymore," replied Hermann.

The major and Forrestal exchanged glances. The major nodded slightly—a knowing expression.

"Major, Private Hermann, I will authorize you both to work directly under my supervision until the President executes his plan for managing this kind of activity. Major, I want the private to attend leadership courses for NCOs. It's evident he is ready. That is all I have for now."

The major and Hermann got up from their chairs. Forrestal put his cup down and shook the private's hand. "Welcome to the team, Private Hermann."

On September 17, 1947, President Truman signed into law the National Security Act of 1947. It authorized the establishment of the United States Air Force, the National Security Agency, and the Department of Defense, making James Forrestal the country's first Secretary of Defense. Secretly, it established Majestic 12 to set policy on matters related to UFOs. This made James Forrestal a lead member of MJ 12. The major and Private Hermann continued to personally report to Mr. Forrestal on a regular basis. Even though he was not qualified to be a courier, Hermann proved to be remarkably valuable to the major, the DoD, and to the efforts and policy of MJ 12. The major was witness to Hermann's extraordinary contributions while interacting with scientists and government contractors. When a researcher would casually ask what kind of technology was being delivered as a container was opened, Hermann would describe the artifact in detail and explain its function. These researchers were high performers in their field, rich with academic accolades, with PhDs in physics, thermodynamics, and aerodynamics. They would be left in utter amazement by Hermann's command of the subject matter, describing heretofore unknown material and equipment.

In the weeks that followed, Private Hermann, still assigned to Roswell but under the supervision of Army Intelligence, demonstrated keen leadership and excellent problem-solving skills. The major continued to covertly deliver components from the wreckage to an appropriate military contractor and research team for inspection and eventual reverse engineering.

As he was doing this, Hermann realized that this behavior and knowledge was a result of the transmission event at Corona. To his consternation, he would be able to recall the special technical knowledge only if a particular item was placed before him. He could not describe anything to the major after leaving said item or without the visual stimulus. Nor was he able to remember what he had discussed with the scientists. Still, Private Hermann continued to display insight in management, communications, and leadership, assisting the major almost effortlessly. Hermann was placed on the fast track to promotion. Not long after Mr. Forrestal was appointed SecDef, the major, endorsed by Mr. Forrestal, promoted Hermann to corporal after only nine months in his new position.

After another nine months, the major got a call from Mr. Forrestal about Corporal Hermann. MJ 12 was receiving reports about Hermann's performance and contributions in reverse engineering the artifacts collected from the Corona and Roswell crash sites. Before long, Hermann was promoted to sergeant. This qualified him as a courier, able to work alone without the major at his side. His performance did not change. The sergeant remained effective in providing scientists and researchers guidance on the artifacts that were delivered.

When the rate of artifact delivery slowed, Mr. Forrestal called Hermann to arrange a meeting in California. A few days later, the Army sergeant and his major met at Muroc Field. There, the SecDef, with papers in hand, informed Hermann and the major that he was authorizing Hermann to transfer to the Navy as an ensign. MJ 12 wanted Edwin Hermann to be an intelligence officer like his mentor, the major. The effective date would be 15 February 1949. Mr. Forrestal also informed the major and Hermann that he would not be meeting with them anymore. He would soon be replaced as Secretary of Defense, and likely removed from the ranks on MJ 12. He thanked both men for their fine work and dedication to duty, and for maintaining secrecy of the activities. He advised that another member of MJ 12 would be the new contact and that the major would get a call very soon to help orient the member. While the major stepped away for a cigarette, Mr. Forrestal confided in the Army sergeant, soon-to-be Navy ensign.

"Sergeant, MJ 12 has been monitoring alien activity closely. Our contacts have determined that no two alien races are alike or have the same intent when it comes to humans. The aliens that crashed at Corona appeared to not be threats to us. The fact that the alien transmitted information to your brain is proof. Our contacts have learned that you are recognized now by other races—races that have nefarious intentions for humans. Be careful."

The sergeant nodded with keen focus.

"Sergeant, I truly admire how you accepted your job and performed with vigor and a high level of attentiveness. I and the rest of the MJ 12 are impressed how well you handled the responsibility that was forced upon you. You will be a fine Navy officer. I would have liked to watch your progress," the Secretary concluded.

Mr. Forrestal paused and moved closer to the NCO. His eyes telegraphed a somberness. Lips were held tight from the gravity of the moment.

"What could take hold of this great man and cause him to behave this way?"

It was the first time Hermann heard the man's voice quiver: *"Edwin,* I will be the first founding MJ 12 member to leave. I don't feel safe. I possess information that is highly sensitive to national security. If I were to be taken by a hostile country, that country would have the potential to cause catastrophic damage not only to the United States but to the free world. I have also demonstrated disagreement on how MJ 12 is using its authority. I think the public deserves to know we are not alone. As I leave office, MJ 12 has a dilemma concerning me. I don't think they trust me to remain quiet. If I don't see you again, remember me as someone that truly cared about you—and about Americans."

Sergeant Hermann's look at the Secretary of Defense changed from attentiveness and respect to grim solemnity. That was the last time Hermann had any contact with Mr. Forrestal.

A few months later, on May 22, 1949, the news reported that James Forrestal's body was found on the pavement, outside the wing at Bethesda Naval Hospital where he was being treated. The official story was that Forrestal, admitted for depression and psychological problems, tried to escape and fell sixteen stories to his death. The window was shown with bed sheets hanging out. Hermann was suspicious of the incident, especially after what the SecDef told him at the last meeting.

From that day, Hermann lost trust in MJ 12. Also, on that day, Hermann and the major received messages that there would be no more contact with MJ 12, and that both were to carry on their work as if they had never heard of MJ 12. They were separately given instructions that they would be contacted by someone with the newly formed National Security Agency. Each man would be assigned his own contact.

The work surrounding the crashes in New Mexico subsided. In the years that followed, there were sightings and more crashes around the world. Hermann's continued role was to investigate, gather information and materials, and assist in reverse engineering efforts as needed. The major remained on active duty for a short while, then retired. Hermann and the major lost contact after the retirement.

Hermann's unrelenting professional performance and leadership earned him promotions to the rank of commander. Throughout his life, he retained the special knowledge and acute wisdom gained from his contact at Corona. There had been moments on assignments to other sightings or crashes that he believed some objects had originated from other races—the ones Mr. Forrestal had warned him about.

* * *

Katrina's father stopped and paused for a while, looking beyond the hills of the cemetery. "Dad? Are you OK?"

Her father nodded and looked at her.

"It's alright, Dad; I understand."

"No," the old man stammered, short of breath again. He turned to face her. His bony fingers gripped her wrist tightly as he raised his voice, "You . . . and your older brother! . . . you both were abducted! Edwin Junior died of cancer from the radiation. You . . . your experiences and abilities occurred from being abducted when you were eleven. He was seventeen."

Katrina was at a loss for words. The jolt she felt from her father's confession masked the pain in her wrist. She looked down at his pallid face and directed her glare to his sunken bloodshot eyes: eyes weary from witnessing too many unthinkable events. In decades past, those same eyes shone with hope. Edwin worked with the belief mankind would eventually benefit from the advanced systems discovered at crash sites. With every passing year, he realized higher authorities had no intention of releasing the technologies to the public. The hope he held on to would be locked away in secret files indefinitely.

Katrina's father let go of her wrist, took out a little brown book, and handed it to her. He began his long-withheld lament.

"This is what I kept from you and your late mother. Keeping it to myself all this time has been a terrible burden. It has made me more ill with every passing day. Your mother fell into dementia and died before I could tell her. Your brother gave this to me before he died. It is his diary. Read it. Start with the bookmarker."

Katrina began to read as her father turned his gaze over the west part of the cemetery's tree-covered hills and stone markers.

Auburn, California

9/28/81

Walking home from town, I noticed a very bright white light illuminating the area.

I felt an attraction to the light. Walking into it, I kept my eyes down, looking at my feet. I sensed movement. I was told to stop. In an instant, I was inside a polished metallic chamber. I found myself in line with other men and women. No real words or conversation took place. The line was moving. Somewhere along the line, my clothes disappeared. Somewhere in the back someone said, "He's too young to mate." I was then taken into a room with what I thought was a stainless-steel operating table. The table had a movable stainless-steel arm rest. Greys were in control of me and what was happening in the room. The few tall blond white men seemed to be posted to security points in walkways and rooms, never saying anything. It was the Greys who talked to me and subdued me at the operating table.

They were strong for their size. I struggled to get free but their fingers were like vice grips. One gripped my left clavicle area, ripping an artery, which caused internal bleeding. They fixed it temporarily and promised to get back to it after they did another procedure. The other procedure was insertion of what looked like a plastic tube under my ribs on my left side. The tube was over an inch wide. The procedures were uncomfortable but without real pain.

After the operation, I was allowed to see the craft I was on. I also saw that there were four other little ships. Soon after, I was back on the ground.

Four of the little ships rose and went into the mothership. They lit a path all the way to my door. Then they were gone.

I am at home now and am very sick. I am having a terrible migraine headache. I am beyond hypersensitive; it is as if I can hear each hair on my head growing out of the scalp. Writing in my book has been like sawing on stone. I have to stop now.

Katrina looked at her father with a look of horror. "Read the next page," he said, pointing to the diary.

Katrina turned the page.

My father called some people today and they took me to the only lab in town. They were able to determine that I was suffering from radiation poisoning. The results were given to my father. He told me to never tell anyone what happened. His only remark was "What in the hell did I get into this time?"

"That's all that is important and what I wanted you to read," said her father as he took the diary from her. After tucking the journal away, he returned his focus to Katrina.

"When Edwin Junior died in 1996, I kept the details of the autopsy secret. You know, he died of a brain tumor. When he was x-rayed, the technician had noticed radiation burns already on his skull . . . old burns. I kept that to myself, concerned that it would raise questions and lead to the truth about the abduction."

Her father paused to allow her to absorb the news and think about it a bit, then added more to her plate.

"I am convinced that your brother was abducted because of my activities when I was on active duty. Later on, I suppressed information from the public and censored reports from Navy and Air Force pilots. Afterward, you were taken, too, but you have no memory of it. You and your brother were contacted by a rogue group of an alien race that intended to enter into a treaty with the United States in the early fifties. Just because one race may be benevolent, doesn't mean that all are benevolent. Just like in humanity, there are criminals among alien populations. The rogue group were mutineers to the rest of their fleet. They wanted to experiment with humans without any order or rules. They were linked to numerous cases of sickness, mental illness, and suicide. You and your brother were targeted because of me. And I turned out to be in Navy Intelligence, working on the UFO cases because of this man." Her father motioned to Forrestal's stone monument.

"When you found Robert, I was relieved you found someone that understood and accepted you. I am satisfied that I will pass knowing you have your life back."

"Robert and I found *each other*," Katrina said, slowly and emphatically. "We both needed some mending."

Katrina's father nodded.

"It's OK, Dad. How would you have known? Who knows what would have happened if you had stayed in?"

There wasn't much to add. Navy Commander Retired Edwin Hermann had fulfilled what he had hoped to accomplish before his passing. His long-held remorse, which acted like an illness, began to subside as they left Arlington National Cemetery to return to the retirement home. Katrina stayed with her father for lunch. After lunch, she sat down with him to have more conversation about better things. Neither one asked questions concerning her unique experiences or his.

"How's your Ranger boyfriend?"

"He's doing well. His security consulting business is growing."

"You seem to attract those type of people, don't you? That's alright. He seems to be good man with a lot of heart."

"Thanks, Dad."

"I was pleased to find out that you left Nevada—too close to Grass Valley."

"And I'm satisfied that you found this place to your liking. Dad, how much did you know about what I could do with my mind?"

Edwin jerked toward the seat back as if something hit him. "I only know what you did at the house, and for both of our safety, I preferred not have any other knowledge. And I would like it to remain that way, just as you should not learn about the details of my work, beyond what I told you today."

Katrina often wondered how much he knew of her activities since she moved out of his house. She assumed he had probably gotten information from an NSA connection. He had a brother in NSA as well. Spying is nepotistic.

The time passed quickly and Edwin was getting tired and needed a nap. That was Katrina's cue to leave for good. Emotions and hugs were not common in the Hermann household, at least not with a military father who could not separate his rank from his family. Katrina still found it difficult to forgive his harshness with her mother, who had suffered greatly from severe arthritis and, later, dementia. Father and daughter both understood this would likely be their last meeting, yet the goodbye was casual and unaffectionate.

Katrina left for Taos the following morning, pleased her father was able to release himself from the guilt of keeping the secret. She also appreciated his telling her about his contact at Corona.

2

... HER OWN APOLOGY

On the flight home, Katrina tried to nap but couldn't stop thinking about her visit with her father. He hadn't allowed her the opportunity for one final act of affection. Had she prevented him from opening up to her? No. No. It was him. Katrina was angry at herself for hoping that he had changed.

Katrina arrived in Santa Fe late at night after a layover in Dallas. Although she had been gone only a couple days, she was relieved to talk to Robert as they rode back to Taos. She discussed her trip to Washington, DC, the details about her father, the Corona crash, and Secretary of Defense Forrestal. Robert still had difficulty understanding Katrina's psychokinetic ability. He had even more difficulty believing anything related to UFOs and extraterrestrials. It made him uneasy. The thought of other races coming to Earth at will and the government suppressing the information from public channels terrified him almost as much as his memories of Iraq and Afghanistan. Katrina did not dwell on the sensitive topics and respected Robert's views and beliefs.

Once home, she checked the mail Robert had left on the kitchen counter. Next to the stack of mail was the pad of paper, Katrina's letter to her daughter, still on top. She skipped the mail, picked up the paper, and paused.

"Robert, is there a reason you put the pad with my letter next to the mail?"

"No. I just thought you had forgotten about it," he replied.

Katrina looked at the words she had written. She had been sincere, and the words had poured out from her love for her daughter. She thought about her visit with her father and all the secrets he revealed. Katrina had secrets too, which she had neglected to put in the letter. She knew she needed to tell her daughter more. "I originally thought I'd send her the letter, but now I know I need to give it to her in person," she said as she picked up the phone and dialed.

The phone call surprised Emma. Katrina usually only called on weekends or late at night. "Mom? Is everything OK? Why are you calling me?"

"I'm fine, darling. Well, sort of. I mean, I'm not sick. I just returned from DC, where I visited Grandpa. He's not well. He asked me to visit him one more time."

"How was it?"

"I wish...I wish it had been...better. He told me things I think you should know. I need to talk to you about it in person, face-to-face. There is a lot to tell you that both I and you did not know about Grandpa."

"I would love to see you, Mom!" Emma said, ramping up the emotion in the hope Katrina would visit. "When can you come for a visit? Summer?"

"I was thinking...next week?"

Emma was caught off guard by Katrina's request. It was difficult enough to be around her mom when she had time to prepare for it. She felt her long-distance excitement recede like a quickly departing tide. The silence was awkward.

"Emma, it is important I see you as soon as I can, while thoughts are still vivid in my mind."

"Um, OK then. See you next week, Mom," Emma said, the eagerness returning to her voice. She really wanted to see her mom.

* * *

Emma met Katrina outside the baggage terminal. On the way to Emma's apartment, Katrina updated her daughter on life in Taos with Robert. Emma talked about her work in the neonatal ward. It was approaching 10 p.m., but before letting Katrina retire for the night, Emma wanted more information.

"OK, Mom, you didn't tell me over the phone and we didn't talk about it in the car. What is the real reason you felt you needed to come on such a short notice? Tell me more about the visit with Grandpa."

Katrina found a comfortable place to sit then opened up to Emma about the details from her visit to Arlington National Cemetery. Emma sat, stunned, intent, quiet but with occasional expressions of surprise, incredulity, and simple awe. When Katrina revealed her father had told her she had been abducted, Emma's eyes began to tear.

"It seems so odd that I don't know my own mother as well as I should," her daughter claimed.

"That is really why I am here. After Grandpa bared all those secrets to me, and told me things about myself and my brother that I had never known, I realized that I needed to have the same kind of talk with you before it became too late. Yes, I needed to let you know about Grandpa, but there is also a lot about me that I never told you."

Katrina went to her bag and took out the envelope with the letter she wrote to her daughter. She walked back to the couch, sat down next to her daughter, and handed it to her.

"Darling, I wrote this earlier this week. I was going to mail it to you, and then I got the call to visit Grandpa. When I returned, I decided it would be better to give it to you in person and explain everything, just like he did to me."

Emma opened the unsealed envelope to read the handwritten letter. It made her cry. Katrina also wept.

"Sweetheart, everything that I will tell you now is true. Every bizarre detail, every strange occurrence. I suppose I need to start at the beginning."

3

... HER CHILDHOOD

Katrina was the last of three children. Her older sister, Mavis, teased her incessantly about being the youngest, the "runt," and the "accident." Mavis claimed that by the time she was born, her parents' reproductive organs were so old that Katrina would always be inferior.

In school, Katrina was characterized as a strange girl by the other kids. Her classmates' parents talked about her mysterious father who isolated his family. Her parents never entertained and they rarely attended social gatherings. She conquered the stigma, not by trying to fit in with the normal kids but by rebelling against the popularity cults. She used her wild and off-beat imagination to make the others think twice about teasing or bullying her. She learned this defense mechanism in the early grades and refined it to an art later in her pre-adolescent years. It eventually turned out to be a source of personal entertainment for her. Instead of being the subject of scrutiny and inspection, she put her classmates through her own social experiments. Her imagination and morbid sense of humor terrified them.

If Katrina had been abducted at the age of eleven, she had no recollection of the incident. There was no residual damage. She had no recurring nightmares, no phobias, no mental illness. Perhaps because it had happened at a young age, it did not impact her memory. Not only were there no emotional or mental signs, there were no physical signs or marks on her skin.

At home, her childhood's unhappy memories were from having a father who couldn't separate his military bearing from family life. In Katrina's family, the order of allegiance was military first, followed, in a close second, by God. Because of her father's unique position in the Department of Defense, the family lived in the western part of the United States: Sacramento, Auburn, then Nevada, where her father retired.

Her father was distant, and his words and actions made loving him difficult. He was emotionally abusive to her mother, a nurse, and later, social worker, who was stricken with rheumatoid arthritis early in life. She valiantly continued her full-time work and her chores as military wife and mother without complaints.

One night, Katrina overheard her father tell her mother, "If you were a cow, I'd have you shot." It hurt Katrina to witness her father berate and take her mother for granted. She was just as frustrated about her mother acquiescing to her husband's behavior, and she challenged her mother to stand up for herself. When confronted in that way, Katrina's mother would shrug and change the subject or assign some sort of task to occupy her daughter. The mistreatment would be a lasting memory.

Katrina also recalled the night her father introduced a stranger to the family: Lily. Lily would attend family events, especially during the holidays. She was so regular in her appearances that she was eventually treated as part of the family. Lily was an attorney with the IRS and met her father through an investigation when she was working as a liability consultant with the NSA. Katrina later learned that Lily was her father's mistress. This added another wedge between her and her father. Much to Katrina's consternation, her mother learned to accept the infidelity, blaming herself and her health.

Her relationship with her mother, coupled with witnessing the abuse and infidelity of her father, taught Katrina to be self-sufficient.

4

... HER YOUNG ADULTHOOD

Katrina's sister was partially correct when she teased about her genetic inferiorities. The confirmation came when Katrina began to attend classes at San Diego State. She experienced problems in listening and encountered trouble in focusing on the professors' voices during lectures. She sought help, was tested, and then diagnosed with auditory processing disorder, otherwise known as hearing dyslexia.

She couldn't remember precisely when she began to have problems processing what someone would say to her. She recalled learning to listen intently and having to ask someone to repeat their words. She developed the habit of replying with a "huh?" after someone would talk to her. It added to her peculiarity. Oddly enough, there were a few relatives diagnosed with high function autism. Katrina did not find out about them until her problem was detected.

Her diagnosis provided another trait that placed her in an elite group. Results from the tests also determined she possessed a "genius" level of proficiency in abstract concepts. All this contributed to a most unique health record. Her family doctor took notice and made it a point to monitor her on a regular basis. Katrina recognized it as another instance of her strangeness but certainly apart from what her sister would attribute as a weakness.

Katrina's home in Grass Valley, California, had its own weird character. The town's population in 1990 was no more than 9,000. Katrina felt something was odd about the town. She sensed an absence of a normal level of humaneness and happiness. She had to look hard for a hint of a smile on citizens' faces. She didn't see frowns or anger, just blank looks. She imagined the town was populated by zombies. People would walk past her on the sidewalk and not even look at her face. The more she thought about it, the more it made her curious.

Occasionally, and more often than she thought normal, she would read in the local paper about someone committing suicide. Her mother, a nurse, would come home with stories about doctors' concerns over the high number of people contracting rare forms of cancer. She also heard her mother talk about people going crazy and being taken away. Clearly, she surmised something was not right about the town. She hypothesized Grass Valley was cursed by either the spirits of gold miners from the rush or the spirits of Native Americans. Whatever it was that affected the town's aura of gloom, it made her resent the place more.

Katrina would eventually find out why her town couldn't shake the specter of darkness.

5
... HER ERODED INNOCENCE

Katrina disclosed to Emma that she discovered the ability to use her mind to do astonishing things when she was a freshman enrolled at San Diego State University.

In the 1970s, Soviet scientists experimented with radio and sonic waves on unsuspecting Americans in embassies. The activity caused headaches, nausea, even depression. At that time, the United States was behind in understanding this technology. The experimentation gave the United States intelligence community the opportunity to learn about this kind of weaponry. It prompted a response from the State Department, which set up programs for study.

Coincidentally, not long after the discovery of the experiments, in 1975, the United States Psychotronic Association (USPA) was established. The organization defines psychotronics as the science of mind-body-environment relationship: an interdisciplinary science concerned with the interactions of matter, energy, and consciousness. Psychotronics involves the study, research, and applications of the physics and technology of the mind, brain, spirit, consciousness, and the underlying forces of life and nature.

Katrina realized she had been blessed by the opportunity to go away to college. Though just 500 miles south of her home in Nevada County, San Diego State felt like a different world. It fed Katrina's desire for adventure. Independent and curious, Katrina often drove all over the region around the university, to La Jolla, Miramar, the beaches, Penasquitos, and locations further north.

One day, her gallivanting took her further north of her normal route, and she found herself near Camp Pendleton. Just after noon, she walked into a sandwich shop outside the main gate. After receiving her order, sitting down, and settling into her first bite, she noticed a man looking at her from another table. She looked away and sipped at her drink. He continued to stare at her. She shifted nervously in her seat and sought an exit. She found one, behind her, but she realized she would have to cross paths with him to get to the main exit.

The man got up from his seat, and, without losing eye contact, approached her. Katrina looked away, putting her sandwich down. The man stopped at her table. He invaded her space, taking a seat across from her.

"Hello. I have been waiting for you to show up. My name is Sonny, Sonny Lyle."

Katrina drank from her straw again as an excuse not to speak a word.

"I know what you are thinking and feeling now. You are alone. Suddenly, a complete stranger has approached you after you avoided eye contact," he said calmly. "You feel threatened and you don't know what will happen next."

Katrina finished drinking. "What do you want?"

"Relax. Finish your lunch." The man's order was called. "That's mine. I'll be right back. Don't leave. I actually want to help you."

Katrina recognized she had a chance to bolt from the shop and jump into her car, but something told her to stay. The man returned with his order and sat down again. Unwrapping his meal, he began to explain himself. "I am on a break," said the stranger. She knew his name, but he was still a stranger.

He was fit but not a muscle-builder type, wearing a tight black tee shirt and matching exercise shorts. He looked like he was in his forties, bald, soothing brown eyes, and dark skinned.

"I run a self-defense studio next door. If you come and learn the moves, and more importantly, gain a better sense of confidence and inner peace, you would be able to respond to this situation if I were a threat."

"What makes you think I lack confidence and that I am not able to defend myself?" she asked indignantly.

"Look at your posture."

Katrina straightened herself.

Sonny continued. "Immediately, once I entered this shop, your facial expression and body language told me everything about how you would react if I were a threat. You would benefit greatly from just a few hours of lessons, and my approach is holistic, involving the whole body and most importantly, the *mind*."

"Are you saying that personal defense depends more on mental strength than physical strength?"

"Exactly. It is ancient wisdom. The definition of mind over matter."

"Doesn't it take a long time to attain that kind of discipline? Isn't that what Tibetan monks dedicate their life to learn?" Katrina asked.

"You don't need to be a monk to gather what I will teach you. I will start the process. It will be up to you to nurture what I impart to you."

Sonny devoured his sandwich quickly. He had little time before he had to teach his next class. Curious and aware of her situation, Katrina took up his offer and followed him out of the shop to his studio next door. Sonny mentioned he was a former Air Force major and C-130 pilot. Katrina introduced herself as a full-time student at San Diego State.

The exercise studio was oversized compared to its handful of students. It was a simple open room with floor mats and a wall of mirrors. Katrina took a spot near the modern steel and glass wall that flooded the room with natural daylight.

Her first session went well and she returned for three more sessions, learning the martial art of Chi. She learned that Chi, an eastern discipline, is not just for self-defense. Her instructor professed it was the vital life-force energy of the universe. He maintained that the energy flows through the body at specific points known as chakras. Sonny explained that in order to communicate with the Chi, the students needed to learn to use their minds. They needed to imagine their center of gravity just below the navel. To demonstrate his point, he asked the class to form a group in front of him and try to shove him off his feet. In unison, they applied their strength to move him. They failed the first time. Surprised by the resistance, they put more effort into the push. They failed again. He could not be budged.

In the next three weeks, Katrina learned about using the energy of the opponent to her advantage. Sonny demonstrated how to take advantage of her balance against the perceived imbalance of an attacker, using the attacker's motions to her advantage. Most of all, she learned through practice with an opponent to be confident and mentally secure. Sonny taught only for defense. By the fourth week, she was feeling quite comfortable with the lessons, and it showed.

She demonstrated early progress. Part of the lessons involved meditation, and the past three weeks she not only meditated well in class but also meditated before classes.

It was during the fourth session she experienced a harrowing event that pointed to a special ability. While in meditation, she successfully quieted herself to a different state of awareness, apart from her human form. She found herself detached from her physical self. It was her first out-of-body experience (OBE). She did not feel any mode of travel as the vision of being inside a human body appeared to her. With amazement and alarm, she realized it was the body of her instructor, Sonny.

Another living organism surrounded her. It vibrated. Veins and organs floated around her with no visible structure. She was also suspended over darkness. She was out of body, with no recognizable form. And yet, her temporary cell was real. She had no idea how she had gotten there, and she had no idea how to get out—if there was a way out. It was a most bizarre awareness, sensing his organs, feeling his natural warmth. Now closed in, she could hear the flow of his blood and the beat of his heart enclosing her in a sonic, invisible pulsating shell. To her horror, she heard him instruct her.

Katrina, I feel you. You are inside me. We are one. You are me now. Feel me. All around you. Now listen. You can control me. Listen to the heart. You can slow it down with your thought. I want you to slow it down, down, down, to a stop.

The thought of killing him while her spirit was inside him sickened her. The death wish caused her to scream, startling the class.

Her physical scream worked to disconnect her from the experience, breaking the link, and returning to her body. Once she regained her composure, she stood and ran out of the studio.

She quickly got in her car and raced back to her parents' home in Grass Valley. She would never return.

6

... HER SPIRITUAL INTUITION

Despite the incident at Camp Pendleton, Katrina finished school with an engineering degree in electronics. She found work in a design firm in Sacramento, where she earned a generous salary. She stayed with her parents in order to save money for a place of her own, also allowing her to help in supporting her mother. So much for her intention to lead a normal adult life. It wasn't up to her. Her life's direction had been determined long before she was born.

Although her father retired as a Navy officer when she was a young girl, the military continued to impose its will on him and the family. Other members in the family were involved with the CIA and NSA, so the rumors went. Because of her father's involvement in highly sensitive activity, Katrina's family was constantly under surveillance. But it wasn't only the awareness of being watched that had an effect on her. Intelligence agencies conducted activities beyond eavesdropping and monitoring. They took aggressive actions against Katrina, impacting her day-to-day activities, not allowing her normalcy. They stalked her. They would even contact people she socialized with. Their intrusions caused her to always be on alert, always waiting for some form of harassment or at least an interruption of her effort to have a normal life.

It motivated her to seek out a regular life after graduation. She met a guy, fell in love, and immediately got pregnant. Her parents arranged a wedding prior to the birth of her daughter. Not long after the wedding, her husband took a job in Colorado. She had to quit her steady professional job, following him there to be a housewife and mother. Katrina was miserable and her marriage turned sour. Their personalities caused conflict. He was a former Air Force officer, accustomed to being a leader, and she had grown to be a confident, independent woman. While she contemplated leaving with her daughter, her father called, told her that her brother, Edwin Junior was dying, and said to return home. She took her infant daughter on a plane back to California, leaving her husband. At home, she discovered her brother was dying from a rare brain cancer. Katrina remained, caring for him at their parents' home. Her mother's health was declining as the arthritis ravaged her body. Katrina did her best to help her mother and brother while still raising her infant daughter. She decided she would not return to Colorado to be with her husband.

It didn't take long for her brother to be admitted for palliative care. Katrina visited her brother there, sensing he was approaching his last days. Doctor Eric Garson, the family physician, was surprised to see her.

"Katrina? Why are you here? There is no change to your brother's condition."

"I am here because something tells me he will pass away soon. I think he wants me to be with him when he takes his last breath."

Doctor Garson did not reply. Her response caused him to look at her closely, almost squinting with suspicion. Garson often looked worn, unkempt. As a citizen of the town, he wasn't an exception to being affected by the mental gymnastics associated with his position. In addition, somehow, he gained a habit or trait of batting his eyelids rapidly when he talked. Katrina spoke with little emotion in her voice, as if under a spell. She did not visit out of love. She was summoned, and she intuited that she had *something* to do. It was a healing that no doctor nor nurse could give because it wasn't a healing for his body. Doctor Garson temporarily surrendered his position, stepping aside. He opened the door to the patient's room and yielded to Katrina. Curious and apprehensive, he followed her. She appeared to glide in effortlessly. Even with everything collapsing around her: her mother's failing health, separating from her husband, and now learning that her brother is dying, something suppressed her emotions. She sensed she had a special task to accomplish. Consequently, her face was absent of pain or sorrow, detached from the present, in another realm.

Katrina sat down next to her unconscious brother, reaching for his hand. Garson noticed the curtains at the window begin to flutter and wave, though the window was closed and the air register was not blowing. Katrina felt something like an electric shock coming from her brother's hand into hers, then up her arm and out the top of her head. Quickly, the room became meat-locker cold. Doctor Garson was startled as he witnessed his exhaled breath in the air. Frightened by the supernatural event, he got up to leave in haste. Stopping at the door, he was stunned by the touch of the frosted handle as he unlatched it.

Katrina was not startled by the energy coming from Edwin Junior, shooting up and out of her. She remained by his side and was allowed to grieve in solitude for a while. Leaving the room, she found Doctor Garson leaning against the wall, facing the door, waiting for her. He needed straight answers. Garson held contempt for mysteries that surrounded his patients, as though he had other intentions.

"How did you know your brother was going to die today, at this hour?" he asked.

"I don't know," said Katrina, baffled by it all. "I think he called me through his spirit."

"What happened in there, Katrina?" Garson continued to interrogate instead of console her.

"Doctor Garson, you know as much as I do. This has never happened to me. I..."

Katrina's recollection of the episode at the Chi studio made her stop and feel defensive. She felt threatened by his approach.

"What? What are keeping to yourself? You're not telling me everything. What are you holding back? If you have a secret, I need to know it as your family doctor!"

Katrina remained silent but kept her eyes steady on his beady-eyed, pockmarked face. Garson did not succeed in getting any more information. She understood there was something special about her that she needed to come to terms with. But more importantly, she needed to be discreet and protect herself.

"Katrina, this is a small town," Garson said. "People talk. Eventually, word gets around. Sometimes the people who are talking make things up. I suggest you think about this and decide if you want your life to be upended by gossip or if you prefer people to know the truth."

Garson's statement resembled a threat. Katrina remained silent and her glare did not change. Garson left, frustrated.

Katrina returned home to tell her parents that her brother had passed. Her parents had anticipated and planned for it. The three sat at the kitchen table, and the conversation shifted to Doctor Garson.

Katrina described how he had accused her of having special knowledge because she arrived just as her brother passed.

"First of all, when someone dies, and the family member is there, the doctor is supposed to be sympathetic, having concern for the mental health of the family members. Garson was rude. He insisted I was keeping a secret from him, an ability he thought I had," explained Katrina.

"There are some things you need understand about Garson and this town. Garson is CIA," replied her father in a monotone voice. Katrina's eyes widened from the revelation. "We are near a few bases here. This area is crawling with CIA, and it's because of Beale Air Force Base."

"How long have you known that Doctor Garson was CIA, Dad?"

"On my second visit with him, he asked me questions that were not the kind of questions a family physician would ask. I replied with a question that indicated my suspicions, and he responded by telling me that he was one of the people assigned to watch us and that I had no choice. He actually said that."

"So, it's true. We *are* all under surveillance!" Katrina looked at her mother, who was under medication and displayed an all-too-common vacant expression. She then turned to her father. "Why don't we move to some other place away from the military people?"

"Katrina, don't you think I've thought about this? We will always be under surveillance. There is no place they will not be able to watch us. But just as they are watching us, I have been watching them. I know who they are. I have learned their ways. Some, like Garson, have actually revealed a lot about why they continue to watch us. I am making the best of this situation, and you should too. They mean no harm. It is a matter of national security."

Katrina continued to describe the incident that transpired in her brother's room as he passed. "Dad, you don't know what happened in my brother's room today. I don't even completely know. I went there because I *heard* him tell me to go to him." She further explained that it was the incident that made Garson change the way he talked to her. "Garson thinks I am hiding something from him about myself. How can I hide something about myself if I don't know what is happening to me?"

This made Katrina's mother look at her husband without turning her head as a tear formed in the corner of her eye and rolled down her face. Katrina's father was slow to respond.

"How do you know it was you? What if what happened in the room was because of phenomenon related to your brother's brain cancer? You don't know for certain it was you, do you?"

Katrina continued to vividly recall the incident at the Chi studio, but she shook her head. Inside, she was certain that something was happening to *her*. She did not need to discuss it further; it would have caused more stress for her aging parents. Her father got up to make calls and prepare for the tasks related to taking care of his son's body and arranging the memorial service.

The memorial service was modest, almost hermetic. In addition to not publicly socializing, the family did not attend church. Edwin Hermann believed in God but not the religions. To Katrina's consternation, Garson and a couple strange figures appeared at the chapel, uninvited and unwelcome, and did not offer any consolation to the family. Katrina's father recognized the other men as members of the medical community in town. Katrina asked him why the men were there. He replied dryly that they were there to "keep tabs on us, closing a chapter." Katrina did not want to accept this as a normal part of her existence in town. She refused to be assimilated in what she recognized as a culture of cold shadowing, let alone as the subject under callous manipulators of other people's lives.

Katrina remained in Grass Valley, caring for her mother as she underwent multiple surgeries. In addition, she was able to get her job back with the engineering firm in Sacramento. Her father, retaining the military mindset, left Katrina to work with her mother without any assistance. He spent time writing and rewriting his diary. He also wrote articles in such magazines as *Popular Science* and *Soldier of Fortune*. Not long after the incident involving her brother, Katrina filed for divorce, keeping her daughter, Emma. She would never marry again.

Katrina's father continued to distance himself from any responsibility, which included caring for his stricken wife. Katrina was the prime caretaker. In addition, she was raising Emma, now an active and curious toddler who had developed learning disabilities. All this time, Katrina's mother was devastated that her husband knew of the surveillance, coming to accept that nothing could be done about it. The reality of being under a systematic watch, and not being able to be secure in the family's privacy, worked to erode the bond between family members. As anticipated by Edwin Senior, Doctor Garson put Katrina on the watch list. Garson took her resistance personally, going beyond protocol and policy regarding Katrina. The operatives he knew were sociopaths. They enjoyed inflicting torture. Although not sanctioned by the CIA, these rogue units were not under any control, and there were no repercussions when the units used excessive means in their surveillance activity. Working on an identified CIA testing site made it easy for Garson to devise a plan to physically punish Katrina for her resistance and stubbornness.

Katrina was destined to come to terms with her psychic abilities. The rogue CIA cell, with direction from Garson, determined to force Katrina to find a way to defend herself against unimaginable torture executed by CIA operatives.

7

... HER SELF-INCRIMINATION

Katrina was obsessed by the alarming number of people she perceived to be genuinely unhappy in their small town. The number of suicides and population of people with substance abuse or mental illness never failed to enter into her dinner table discussions. Her own failure in seeking friendship and a relationship with a man led her to doubt lovability.

This caused her to fall into depression—a depression that worsened with every unsuccessful attempt to emerge or battle her way out of it. She eventually had a breakdown, becoming more like the other troubled souls in her town. Katrina's mother recognized her daughter's lethargic state, how she failed to pay attention to her appearance. She advised Katrina to seek help and recommended she make an appointment with Dr. Donald Richards. Richards was well respected in town, especially among other health-care professionals. Katrina's mother knew there was no one more qualified in the town for counseling. Katrina's father did not add to the conversation.

However, Dr. Richards also happened to be a CIA asset. Richards held an ongoing role in documenting the damage and recovery from the 1986 Chernobyl incident in the Soviet Union. Like Garson, Richards showed an interest in Katrina. After her failed marriage, he conspired with other town doctors to make it difficult for her to start a serious relationship with any man. Men avoided her after they were dissuaded by the doctors and CIA operatives. The CIA cell was notorious for making life difficult for nonconformists and were intent on adding to the despair in Katrina's life. Thus, her demeanor degraded to the point where she sought help for depression.

Katrina reluctantly conceded to the visit with Dr. Richards. As she entered his office, she sensed the man behind the desk was not to be trusted. Was her depression causing paranoia? She had little understanding of herself, of what was happening to her mind ... and now she was going to be analyzed? Despite her initial feelings, she had every intention to behave as calmly and normally as possible.

She sat timidly in a chair positioned directly in front of a heavy ornate antique desk. A solitary floor lamp rendered a weak glow to the room that was furnished with heavy curtains, dark carpeting, and dark wood paneling. Katrina recognized that the sound of her voice would die among the overbearing fabric on the floor and walls. She needed to speak assertively. The room's anechoic quality served to make her more aware of every sound, including her uneven breathing. The more she thought about her breathing, the more erratic it became.

Katrina described in detail the path that led to her depressed state.

"Doctor Richards, I'm here because my mother recommended you to treat my depression."

"When did you begin feeling depressed, Katrina?"

"I can't point out exactly when it started. Maybe after my brother died. Everything and everyone around me is dying. I'm surrounded by illness. Nobody is happy in this town! And every day I see my mother, her condition, and how my father mistreats her."

Hearing the doctor scratching notes on his legal pad and hearing the tick-tock of a glass-domed anniversary clock added to her anxiety.

"I miss having friends. I miss being with a guy. I don't understand why it's so difficult to find someone in this town."

Richards had no responses. Katrina began to feel exposed and more uneasy with every motion of his pen. He was rendering, in ink, her deepest private feelings, her ex-husband, and her family. She suddenly regretted being cooperative and open. Then the doctor proved to her that her feelings about this encounter were genuine and not a betrayal. She sensed a message, but the psychiatrist was not speaking. Peering over his glasses, he stared at her intently.

"Katrina, judging from what you have told me, and my prognosis, you have two choices. If you continue to live the way you do: A, you could die, either self-inflicted, or by stress; B, your mental state will slowly wither away to a point of no return and you will fall uncontrollably into insanity. No one will be able to catch you."

Katrina, in a rushed emotional reaction, replied rebelliously, "How about C, none of the above?"

Richards looked at her sternly and then smirked. "So, you heard that? Well done, Katrina. I was advised you were special. Unfortunately for you, but fortunately for us, revealing yourself will be your biggest mistake."

"Oh, so you are CIA too? Is this whole damn town CIA? What the hell! Do you think I'm some sort of threat? That I'll work for some enemy state? I didn't ask for this. I don't know how I got this, and I don't know how to control it. I don't know how to hide it." Katrina made sure to not show any sign of weakness.

"Exactly! You...have...no...control! THAT is the problem! Not having control of such a powerful ability means you certainly ARE a national security risk!"

Katrina slumped back in the chair. She realized nothing else she could say would matter anymore. An ugly horrible thought crossed her mind, to which Richards replied, "No, we won't kill you. You are worth more to us alive than dead. We are interested in your abilities. We want to test you. To find your limits, your range, your sensitivity, and your weaknesses."

The way he read her mind stunned her.

"Now, you can be submissive, and we will be as gentle as possible with you, or you can resist, in which case we will apply pain to your experience—pain like you have never felt before—actually more like torture. The ones that will test you will be pleased to know they can apply their sadistic skills. They are a little sick that way, but the CIA loves to have people like that in the ranks. We carry out our orders without prejudice or reservations. It is less messy that way."

"So, there *are* mad doctors in the CIA, just like the movies, huh?"

Dr. Richards was not amused. He detested a rebellious patient. "We are done here, Katrina. You may leave. Expect changes in and around your house soon. If you notice odd activity, it is us. Don't try to move to another location. If you cross us, you will wish you were dead."

Katrina got up from the chair and left without another word. She spoke of her experience to no one. No sense in endangering the whole family. She was angry at herself for surrendering and agreeing to the visit, for being tricked into exposing her psychic ability to Richards. So many thoughts crossed her mind. Richards would surely tell others about her. Her carelessness now placed her in further danger. The potential for a normal life was gone for good.

She had crossed into a domain to which she would be accustomed for the rest of her life.

* * *

A couple days after the visit with Dr. Richards, Katrina and her parents awoke to the sounds of truck engines near their house. Dark blue step vans without company logos ferried men who appeared to be exterior electricians. Katrina's father did not like what he saw. "Looks like our friends are stepping up their game," he said, his voice ominous. "Those are not telephone company linemen in those unmarked trucks. It seems that they may be changing how they watch us. Well, I'm fine. I am not doing anything illegal. What about you, Katrina? Does this have something to do with you?"

Katrina knew without doubt the activity was all about her. She remained quiet, holding in the secret as long as she could. The men worked on the lines for about half the day. Katrina and her family didn't notice any impact on them that day. The following day, there was more unusual activity. This time, it appeared that workers were installing speaker-like boxes on the existing telephone poles. Katrina's father did not recognize those devices, which made him uncomfortable. He was not used to not knowing.

While Katrina was at her job, Edwin Hermann decided to call his doctor confidant, Garson. It was a short phone call. Garson told Katrina's father that he knew nothing about it. He categorically denied any knowledge of an increase in the surveillance of the Hermanns. Katrina's father was upset. He reasoned that denial is admittance but not disclosure.

As Katrina stepped through the front door after her day at work, the unmistakable sound of rotors permeated the air and grew in intensity. A helicopter approached the house. "What the...!" gasped her father.

Katrina was visibly shaken by his reaction. The sound prompted her mother to leave the bedroom and caused her toddler daughter to cry from fear. Katrina immediately rushed to the baby's room to tend her daughter. The helicopter hovered low and remained in the vicinity for a while. Walls vibrated and windows rattled. Neighbors rushed from their homes to see what was happening. Assembled on their front lawns, the people began to point at Katrina's family home. They gathered in small groups to speculate who had earned the flyover and what they must have done. Edwin stepped outside to dismiss all the attention.

"Go back to your own lives, people," he said with a flip of the wrist.

After the helicopter left and her daughter had quieted, Katrina walked on shaky legs into the kitchen to get a drink for little Emma. Along the way, she passed through the living room where her father was now standing. He had been waiting all day. "You need to tell me what happened at the psychiatrist's office. This new activity is not about me and not about your mother. What are you involved in?" he asked, his tone straightforward, his question accusatory. "Is it about something that happened at school? I know you have some idea why this happening. If you don't tell me, I will find out through my channels." Her father's mind was racing with wild thoughts based on his own experience within the intelligence community.

"You're right, Dad. It's me." Katrina stopped short of adding any detail. "This is MY problem. I did not interact with anyone that I shouldn't have, OK? It is all about me. It is about something I did when I visited Edwin Junior as he died. He contacted me telepathically, or I heard him somehow tell me he was going to die. When he did, as I held his hand, his spirit or some kind of energy shot up my arm into my body and out through my head. Garson was there and saw everything. He peppered me with questions I couldn't answer. I made him upset so he must have reported me. Dr. Richards, another one of your CIA 'friends,' was worse. He tricked me by sending me a message telepathically. When I received it, I was shocked by the choices he was giving me—death or insanity. I told him I chose neither. I should have been quiet. I shouldn't have acknowledged his messages. It's me. I don't know what they intend to do. Richards said, if I try to move away, they will find me and make it worse for me."

Her father turned to look out the window where he could see the devices on the poles nearby.

"Dad, don't get involved in this. These people are sick. They like to torture people. You are no match for them. Times are different from when you were working with them."

Hermann remained fixed on the view out the window as he replied.

"You are my daughter. I still can think and plan. I know how to assess the situation. I still have resources I can reach for help. And I will exhaust every means to give you relief."

... HER SELF-INCRIMINATION

"Dad, you may think you still have friends in the agencies," Katrina carried on. "But they retired just like you. They have been replaced by soulless sadistic monsters. This town is not normal. We've had high numbers of suicides, alcoholics, people that are mentally ill, and high numbers of people dying of strange cancers. This town is not the same as when you and Mom moved here. The things going on here are straight out of the Twilight Zone. We are all a bunch of lab rats. They don't care about the implications. They have no conscience. They have no remorse for pain and suffering they inflict on innocent people."

Still, her father remained silent for twenty seconds ... thirty seconds ...

Katrina figured he had heard enough. Then, while continuing to gaze out the window, he spoke up. "Actually, this town IS normal for a town near certain military installations. Go to any base that houses intelligence operations and you will find, nearby, a small community that has been identified as a CIA test site for one thing or other. Often, those towns are geographically isolated, in a very strategic way."

"Wait, you knew about this place? And you continued to live here?"

"I was not concerned about any impact on us, Katrina."

"I don't believe I'm hearing this! You were a Navy intelligence officer, and you just let things continue without trying to make a change—for your family? Damn! So how about now, Dad? Haven't you heard and seen enough? Mom comes home every day with stories about rare cancers. How do you explain Edwin Junior's rare brain cancer?"

Katrina's question hit a nerve. She realized it, and it caused her to catch her breath and pause. She wished she could take back the remark about how his only son had just died. Her father quietly left the room for his study and closed the door. Katrina remained, looking out the window. The workers continued to climb the poles and install the boxes and cables. Soon, she would understand what Richards was telling her.

8

...HARASSMENT AND TORTURE

The equipment installed throughout the neighborhood was activated the next day. Katrina, home from work, was helping with the dishes after dinner when she sustained her first experience as the target. It involved various degrees of torture, starting with a continuous hiss in her ears, comparable to the noise heard from a speaker connected to a live sound system, on high volume without music. Although distracting and annoying, she felt no discomfort nor pain.

The hiss continued throughout the work week, three times a day and lasting approximately thirty minutes. All the while, her parents were not aware of the activity. She preferred to keep the matter to herself. Then, a couple of weeks later, she was greeted in the evening by higher volume of hissing. It masked subtle sounds around the house, and she found herself asking her parents to repeat things when they spoke to her. The hiss continued throughout the evening and all night, into the morning. She was able to escape it only when she left home for work. Even though she displayed difficulty hearing, her parents continued to be unaware of the electromagnetic harassment of their daughter. The hiss became a routine part of her night for a couple more weeks, more a nuisance than torture.

One day, returning from the grocery store, Katrina noticed unfamiliar vehicles fitted with machines that looked like portable generators. She noticed an emblem on a sticker that indicated the vehicles came from the Department of Energy (DOE). Once home, she described what she had seen and asked her father if he knew what the DOE would be doing in the neighborhood.

"DOE is here and they are setting up generators? Here, in Grass Valley?"

Her father knew that DOE assets were rare and used sparingly for special projects and cutting-edge technology. "Someone has placed you on a unique list, and for this all to occur so quickly is remarkably alarming to me."

His words did nothing to calm her. Katrina concluded it was an ominous sign of the start of another phase of the harassment.

The hissing continued every night, all night. Her tormentors were gracious enough to spare her over the weekends, as though they'd treated her absorption of the hissing as a full-time Monday-through-Friday job. She needed to mask the sound, so she made use of earphones to listen to music on her portable device.

Weeks passed before Katrina sensed a different, more sinister sound in her mind. The hiss was replaced by a constant, louder, low hum. The earphones were ineffective at masking the invasive sound; her tormentors had apparently noticed her use of listening devices and adjusted the noise to punch below the belt, beneath their blocking range. The sound became a source of discomfort, then it started to impact her health. It interfered with her sleep pattern. The constant drone gave her headaches. After a couple sleepless nights followed by miserable, ineffective days at work, Katrina sought help with over-the-counter sleeping pills, despite fearing it would put her on cyclical path of chemical dependency.

The impact was swift and devastating. After a week of struggles to remain alert and awake at her job, she decided to quit. She lied to her parents and said that she had been laid off for lack of work at the firm. She held everything to herself, keeping her parents insulated from any sign that would give them a clue of what was happening to her. She preferred to not add to her mother's already stressful and painful day-to-day existence.

Now at home, with no job, Katrina endured the constant low, loud hum. Her headaches increased in intensity. Signals eventually accompanied the pain—beeps, high pitched constant tones, and oscillating sounds. Confusion began to reign over her. She was unable to determine if the sounds were causing her the head pain or if it was a separate activity. It started to affect her just as Richards described. She began to doubt her sanity. She had fleeting suicidal ideations.

Realizing she was quickly losing the battle, she decided to rally and fight. She made efforts to meditate, strengthening herself mentally and spiritually. Eyes closed, she shut herself off to everything around her, only focusing on her breath. She was disciplined, intensely still, reduced only to her own spirit. As her meditations increased in time and intensified in depth and effect, she could visualize who was behind the controls that enabled the constant torture. At first, she didn't know what to think about the images that appeared in her mind's eye. In time, she was able to identify a small laboratory containing esoteric electrical equipment and trace the source of the low hum to one of the pieces of equipment. Katrina also thought she recognized one of the individuals in the lab, Eli Loom, another town doctor. She reasoned that the lab was in the vicinity. Katrina visualized Loom sitting in what looked like a dentist chair, wired into one of the devices. She envisioned his every move then realized she was able to *hear* his thoughts. He was thinking mostly about Katrina and the effect this experiment would have on her.

Katrina began to take large amounts of acetaminophen in preparation for the torture. She detected Loom thinking that eventually she would die from all the torture and activity they were putting her through. He was unsure how she continued to survive the barrage of electromagnetic pulses.

During one of the sessions, while focusing on the lab, she scanned the room and found a telephone with a pre-printed label on the receiver: BAFB. *Beale Air Force Base,* she reasoned, since Beale was only about fifteen minutes away. Her ability to *see* the images and Dr. Loom's activities helped her maintain her sanity. Listening to his thoughts about suicide and death motivated her to continue her increasingly fierce resistance.

Nevertheless, the electro-persecution continued. It was almost automatic. The activity allowed her to *see* the images, once she focused. Katrina continued to read Loom's mind, the impact now producing a welcomed boomerang effect. It was as if *he* was approaching insanity now. She was able to hear his thoughts clearly.

"Katrina should be pleading for her life by now! I don't understand! No one has endured this much without surrender. She should be having attacks of anxiety and sleeplessness. I am going to recommend we increase the frequency on the pulses."

Her defiance was having a psychological effect on Doctor Loom.

The sessions continued with a stronger intensity, occurring every hour, on the hour, in fifteen-minute durations. With the top of the hour came greater pain. Katrina remained resilient since she was able to witness the expressions of incredulity on the faces of her tormentors in the lab. She heard other thoughts.

"Who is she?" wondered one of the lab technicians.
"How is she still alive?" wondered another.

The antagonistic doctors, undercover CIA operatives, deemed Katrina a superhuman freak. The staff had never encountered anyone like her. They hadn't anticipated someone capable of putting up such a fight.

"Dr. Loom—who is she? How did you find her?"

"Dr. Garson discovered her. He told me she knew when her brother would die. He saw her make the room where her brother lay turn into a freezer."

"My God! She could be a tremendous asset for us!"

"No! She is dangerous! Dr. Richards examined her. She has no control and she is hostile."

"And so, you are trying to kill her?"

"We can't have her roaming around the town, free. She clearly has no idea what she can do. *We* don't even know what she can do and I am not sure I want to find out," said Loom as the technician looked at the data incredulously.

"She's too dangerous. I am going to have to eliminate her," thought Loom.

Katrina plainly read his mind. She was now fearful. She was in eminent danger and did not know what to do.

The following day, an even stronger barrage of pulses blasted Katrina. This time, her entire head felt as if it was vibrating. The pain increased to the point that she felt like the hemispheres of her brain were separating down the middle. She increased the dosage of her acetaminophen. The sessions continued on the hour. Katrina endured the pain but would not die. As the pain increased, so did her telepathic ability . She traced the source of her problems to a lone satellite link. The images became clearer and her range more powerful with the increase of energy applied to her.

By the end of the day, Katrina was exhausted, mentally and physically. She couldn't bear having to go through the same thing for consecutive days without end. She was dealing with a malevolence she never could have imagined, a level of evil she did not think was allowed to exist in civilized countries. She felt like a lab rat at the mercy of an institutional brutality or a hostage in a psychic darkness.

The continual assault drove Katrina to desperation. She needed to escape. "I have to leave," she told her parents, who were well aware of her grievous discomfort now but completely ignorant of the causes for it.

The following morning, before dawn, she packed essentials into her Jeep and headed for Lake Tahoe with baby Emma. She had no plans. She didn't even know anyone there. It didn't matter when fleeing insanity.

As they crossed over a deep canyon on Route 20, about forty-minutes into the trip, a dark gray helicopter without markings rose from the gorge. Its presence startled Katrina, causing her to swerve out and back into her lane. The copter flew alongside her SUV, and the pilot glared at her through his side window. She momentarily turned her head to face him, catching his menacing grin. The pilot positioned the craft to hover over her vehicle, then slowly dropped down on the metal roof. The copter's weight combined with the contact of the steel skids on the roof resulted in a violent scraping sound: a thousand sharp metal fingernails on the chalkboard, just above her head. Emma screamed and cried in terror.

The rotors' movement transferred vibration, causing Katrina to feel the steering wheel rumble. Her tires squealed and smoked as the pilot skillfully applied the copter's weight to the top of the roof. It forced her to brake, decelerating to a crawl. The pilot lifted the helicopter off again and swung it around to face her, hovering just above the pavement, blocking her route. Katrina was stopped and confined.

A man in a suit, sitting in the co-pilot's chair, turned to her and wagged his finger at her as they continued to hover low enough to impede her progress. As she halted, the engine idling, her arms shaking from the terror, she heard a voice on a loudspeaker. "Katrina Hermann! Turn around and go back home—immediately!"

Emma continued to cry uncontrollably. Her mother was frazzled, approaching her limit. Demoralized and defeated, she maneuvered the car toward the center median on the shoulder, stopped, and shut off the ignition. Smoke from the abused tires permeated the scene as she exited the vehicle. Still trembling from the incident, she walked to the back door, opened it to her crying daughter, unbuckled her and lifted her out to hold her close. The helicopter continued to hover above, close enough to almost drown out Emma's crying. Katrina reached into a bag on the passenger seat for a bottle of water and gave it to her daughter to help console her. They stayed outside the vehicle. Katrina held her daughter, soothing her with her soft voice, sitting on a guardrail. Her soft approach and tenderness quieted the little girl, who would occasionally look up at the copter, causing her to hold on to Katrina tighter.

Several minutes passed after Emma stopped crying. Katrina spoke to her tenderly as she placed her back in her seat. Katrina glanced up at the copter as she sat in the driver's seat and started the engine. She drove to the nearest turnout to head back to Grass Valley. The helicopter followed her back until she was off Route 20. The episode drained her, but she was able to return without further incident.

***

"Wait! Mom!" Emma stopped Katrina from continuing her story. "The helicopter...That explains why I have a fear for those things!"

"You still don't like them?" asked Katrina.

"No! I still get nervous when hear or see them."

"I'm so sorry, darling. There's so much more to tell you," Katrina said apologetically.

***

Katrina rued walking through the front door of her family home. It was a sign of failure and her opponent's victory: a deep and personal defeat. Cradling her exhausted daughter closely, she avoided eye contact with her parents, going straight to her room. Her surprised parents were relieved to have her and Emma back. Katrina sheltered in her room, playing with Emma even as the harassment and torture resumed. She took comfort holding her young daughter close to her.

The electromagnetic attacks resumed. So did Katrina's resistance and ability to pick up vital information. She gathered data, healed, regathered data, healed again, and continued to improve, exercising the full power of the human brain to heal itself. Katrina's brain was special and its powers were just as special. The activity allowed Katrina to hear more. Her psychic senses sharpened in accuracy and clarity. She now pinpointed the locations of generators and the sources of energy. She heard conversations, not only in the lab, but outside and in separate conferences. She gained a knowledge of the people assaulting her brain. She learned of their philosophy.

She learned one of the lab technicians actually felt sorry for her and cared for her.

As a way to keep her mind sharp, Katrina applied labels to each person that worked in the lab. She named the one that cared for her Doctor Robert, because he listened to Beatles songs on his portable player. Another technician had a preference for Indian food. She named him Som, after a person she knew in college. She heard herself described her as a dangerous phenomenon that needed to be eliminated, though assassination was tabled as a last resort. They continued to collect data on her. Experimentation was more important, and there was no concern about collateral damage. It was part of their sociopathic make up. She heard them mention a new phase in the experiment that would increase the energy with which she was being bombarded.

The following day marked the beginning of yet another phase of hourly torture. During the first session, early in the morning, Katrina continued to experience an increased sharpness in her senses. The pain was also at a higher level. As soon as they reduced power to end the hourly session, she felt a horrible sensation she had never felt before. Her spine began to feel like it was burning from its core. It was too much. The energy knifed through her with thousands of bits of microelectromagnetical shrapnel, hitting and penetrating her body at high velocities. She screamed and thrashed about, finally curling into a fetal position, crying and sweating profusely. It was so unbearable, she vomited. Hearing the commotion, her parents rushed to her room. They were helpless as she tried to explain what she was feeling. Her mother reached for a phone to call 911, but Katrina begged her not to.

"It's our own doctors who are involved in this, Mom! Garson, Richards and Loom. They all are part of this evil!" she cried. "I can't let them know they are succeeding! Besides, no one is going to help. It may even be a way for them to get rid of me."

Katrina wailed and spewed through her words. The sharp pain slowly subsided, giving her a little time to collect herself before the next of seven more hourly episodes. With every end came the same excruciating sensation. This time, she thought, suicide seemed a suitable option, but still she persisted. That evening, she closed herself in her room, meditated, then organized her thoughts. After a while, she returned to the living room to talk to her father.

"Dad? I have a question."

"What is it?"

"Where is the nearest Russian consulate?"

USN Retired Intelligence Officer Edwin Hermann, a man who'd spent his career as part of a military force dedicated to fighting the Russians and viewing them as the perpetual enemy, looked at his daughter—not as a traitor, though, as a concerned father. Although under Boris Yeltsin, the Russians were not the adversaries that Hermann dealt with, he still harbored some ill will. He knew what was on her mind. Despite her attempts to hide her torture from him, Hermann was aware of the torture she had been enduring recently. He also knew who was behind it. He understood Katrina had little choice. Although it pained him to think of her defecting, especially to the Russians, her intentions were warranted.

"San Francisco, Green Street—Pacific Heights." Her father paused. "You can try, but the Russians may not think you are worth the trouble you may invite. They don't take our damaged goods, Katrina. You are damaged and dangerous."

Katrina's mother wept alone on the couch, not saying a word.

"Dad! What are my choices? What would you do?" Katrina's frustration again moved to anger. "You saw me clenched and contorted in pain on the floor. I am not going to wait here for them to hit me with their energy weapon and feel that burning again. I am leaving early tomorrow with Emma and will ask for asylum from a government that willfully tortures its citizens who possess special abilities."

She made the best of what might have been her last night in the United States. She spent time with her mother, telling her she would call her once she knew her fate. Edwin Hermann had had multiple encounters with the Russians and the consulate. He intimately knew how they operated, what they were after, and how they would go about getting it. His experience told him that his daughter would not interest them. They rarely took on projects. Like their designs of fighters, they used American assets to make their work easier, not more difficult.

"You will be back, Katrina," Edwin said as he retreated to his study.

9

... THE RUSSIANS

The next morning, before being subjected to the electronic bombardments, Katrina took her daughter in her parents' car, in order not to draw attention, and drove straight to the Russian Consulate in San Francisco, about a two-and-a-half-hour drive. The building, an ornate Italianate Revival edifice, occupied half the block. As she walked toward the entrance, she felt a tinge of anxiety. She realized she was walking into yet another situation that presented critical, unknown consequences to her and Emma. Pausing with her hand on the door, she recalled what her father had told her before retiring for the night: *"You'll be back."* She surmised there were as many reasons for her not to walk through those doors than to take the fateful steps.

With that, she opened the door and found herself inside the building. It seemed too easy.

She timidly approached a receptionist.

"May I help you?" asked the woman as she rose from her seat at a large ornate desk.

Katrina looked at her then her daughter, then back to the receptionist. "I request asylum. I declare that I am defecting."

The receptionist cocked her head a bit and glanced at Emma in Katrina's arms. She left her desk momentarily and returned with a young, well-dressed man. He asked Katrina to follow him past a set of controlled doors into a hallway where they entered a small interrogation room. He spoke perfect English. He offered her a drink. Katrina asked for water for her and her daughter, who was behaving well. The man introduced himself as a member of the consulate and screener.

After the introduction, he asked for her personal information. She wrote her name, birth date, address, place of birth, and nearest living relatives.

"Miss Katrina, we need to know why you are asking asylum. Are you a fugitive?"

"No, no," she quickly replied. "I am being harassed by federal agents and do not feel safe here."

"How are you being harassed?"

"I am being attacked by an advanced energy weapon that injures the brain."

The agent looked at her briefly then looked at the child on her lap and paused. Katrina was conscious of having given so much personal information to a potentially hostile entity. Technically, she was not on US territory. He took the information and, leaving Katrina with Emma for a while, passed it on to a staff member to deliver for a background check. He got up to excuse himself and left the room again. This time, he was gone for a longer time. When he returned, he instructed Katrina to go back to the lobby where the seating was more comfortable while her records were being reviewed. The lobby was sumptuously furnished. A wall was adorned by the portraits of notable historic Russians such as Tchaikovsky and Tolstoy. A photograph of President Boris Yeltsin was displayed by itself on another wall. She waited and waited patiently with her toddler daughter; the hours ticked away until three hours had passed.

Finally, ornate Italianate wood doors opened, and an older man with a trimmed beard and mustache, also in a suit, walked into the lobby and went directly to Katrina to sit across from her.

"Ms. Hermann, my staff has completed their review of your records. Why do you wish to seek asylum in Russia?" the man asked in a low, soft tone. He spoke with a slight Russian accent, his English clearly inferring he talked with Americans regularly.

"I am being harassed by the government and I feel my life is in danger." Katrina seemed to stutter.

"How are they harassing you?"

"They are using some kind of advanced energy weapon on my brain."

"And why do you think your government is doing that?" he inquired.

Katrina paused. "I have certain abilities," she said, leaving out detail.

"Certain abilities? Ms. Hermann, you need to be more open with us. Please, what kind of abilities do you have which concerns your government?"

"I ... am clairvoyant."

The Russian looked at her and adjusted himself in the chair to be at her eye level. "Ms. Hermann, there are many, many Americans with that ability. Surely there must be more than you are telling me."

"I ... can do things with my mind. I am able to see things happening at long distances. I can sense what people are thinking."

"Can you tell me what I am thinking?" asked the Russian, knowing the response.

"No. I ... don't seem to have control of it. It comes and goes."

The Russian nodded slowly. "You live in Grass Valley, yes?"

Katrina nodded. "Yes, they said they will either kill me or make me go insane." Katrina trembled slightly as the words left her mouth.

"We are familiar with the area," the Russian replied assertively.

"It's a CIA testing area," Katrina said.

The Russian didn't seem surprised by Katrina's response. "Why do you think they are trying to kill you?"

"I have heard them say that I am a threat."

"Why do you think you are still alive?"

"They want to continue to experiment on me to see what it would take to kill me. I can't go through another day of their torture."

"What do you think will happen to you in Russia? Do you believe you could lead a normal life?" the Russian official asked, maintaining a friendly tone. "Don't you think my country's intelligence agency would have interest in you?"

Katrina felt her face flush. *Perhaps*, she thought, *this was not a good idea.* She remained silent.

The Russian spoke bluntly. "Ms. Hermann, you must realize that right now, sitting here, with your child, you are in Russia. Technically, you have left the United States."

The Russian took in a breath as he looked at Katrina and her daughter.

"It's not so much you want to be in Russia as you want to leave the United States. You fear for your own life. Accepting you to my country would upset our American hosts. Not having control of an unknown superhuman ability is a threat to any country. I'm sorry. You are not worth the risks. I must ask you to take your child and leave. Go back to your parents' home. Your father knows what is best for you."

The last statement startled Katrina.

The Russian got up from his chair and waited for Katrina to stand, take her daughter, and leave. She avoided looking back at him. Fear propelled her to make a hasty exit from the foreign territory in the middle of San Francisco. She felt defeated again. Twice, she had tried to escape. Twice she was stopped.

As anticipated, her father unceremoniously acknowledged her return. Katrina went to her room, composed herself, and sought another way to get out of the daily mental attacks.

10

... SYMPATHETIC SOCIOPATHS

A new day meant only more harassment and torture to Katrina. She endured more burning, more headache, more micro-sized stabs emanating from her spine and traveling through her nervous system.

Katrina was desperate for help. She thought of Sonny Lyle, the Chi instructor from Camp Pendleton. Aside from the CIA scientists disguised as community doctors, he was the only other person who knew of her ability. She remembered her abrupt departure from his studio after his highly irregular dare. What would his reaction be if she called? It would be worth it if it meant getting *something* from him. She rationalized the worst would be no different than the eventual outcome if she did not seek his help.

She hopped online, and learned Sonny Lyle was teaching self-defense in Monterey, California. She called the number for his studio. He answered, and to her surprise, and relief, had not forgotten her.

"Hercules Martial Arts Studio, Sonny Lyle speaking."

"Hello, Sonny? This is Katrina Hermann."

"Katrina! Where have you been? How are you?"

"Oh good—you remember me."

"Of course! Your exit was unforgettable."

"I'm so sorry. I was scared. I had no idea what to do. It was terrifying!"

Katrina did not let Sonny reply. She rushed into the reason she had called him.

"I hope you can help me. I think you are my last chance in a fight against scientists who are using electronic equipment to torture me." Her voice trembled as she rushed through the words. "They are ... they are trying to kill me. They are experimenting on me. It's making my brain feel like it wants to burst through my skull! My spine burns. I feel so many sharp pains throughout my body."

"Slow down. Take deep breaths, just like I taught you."

Katrina did as Sonny instructed. After a few deep breaths, she continued in more calm voice.

"Sonny, I thought that since you recognized my abilities, you might be able to help me control them and use them to fight back."

"If you stayed in the self-defense classes, you would have been better prepared."

Katrina did not respond.

"Who is doing this to you, Katrina?"

"They are CIA scientists posing as town doctors here. I learned the whole town is one big experiment site for them. It's not right what they are doing to the people in this town."

"You're right. It's not. And they should only be doing that work for national security, not for their own self-interests. They need to be stopped."

"So you will help me?"

"I'll will do as much as I can. You said you can't control your abilities?"

"Yes. Things have happened and I don't know why. Just like what happened in your studio."

"Alright. Anyway, I think I owe you this favor. Let's make a plan for you to come to my studio here and stay awhile, OK? This time I won't do anything to terrorize you."

The call ended shortly after Katrina accepted his invitation. She hung up with a touch of hope.

After deciding to leave her daughter with her parents to indicate to her observers she was not trying to flee, she set off to try and solve her problem. Sonny lived on the first floor and kept his studio in the walk-out basement. He met her outside and guided her to a forecourt off the street, where they sat and talked. He invited her to stay at his place, assuring he would be a gentleman. Katrina accepted the accommodations. She detailed the harassment, followed by the energy attacks and the pain. Sonny was angered by the senseless acts of persecution Katrina endured. Recalling their last encounter, he would had preferred for it to have ended better.

"I'm sorry I scared you. I shouldn't have done that to you. It was an indefensible provocation. Your energy actually invigorated me when I felt it."

"I was horrified! Imagine. I had never ever had such an experience before. That was quite a way to learn about it," replied Katrina.

"I'll make it up to you with as much help as I can," Sonny said, his interest and tone a welcome comfort. "There must be a way for you to be able to defend yourself with the abilities you have. After we talked on the phone, I called some friends familiar with the psychic phenomenon you possess. They were intrigued and want to meet you to hear more. They also suspect that what is happening to you in Grass Valley may not be sanctioned by the CIA. There are many rogue units around the world composed of people that were originally recruited for their psychological makeup. Deep down, they are sociopaths."

Sonny waited for Katrina to take in that information. When she seemed to settle, he explained further. "You see, one of the CIA's dirty little secrets is they recruit people who have no regret for killing or injuring other people. Equally disturbing is that they believe they are exempt from obeying the law. Recruiting people like them make assassinations, torture during interrogation, and questionable methods of surveillance more possible. The problem is that eventually those people become difficult to manage. As a weak response, CIA leadership distance themselves and stop giving them support. Many of them continue with their own missions even after the CIA has determined they violated rights and liberties. We believe you are likely a victim of one of those rogue cells."

"OK, so now what?" Katrina asked.

"I have arranged a meeting with some folks that share an interest in your situation and would like to see rogue cells outlawed. Tomorrow we will go through some mental lessons. Maybe we'll do an extended deep meditation. Then we can prepare for a trip to meet my colleagues."

Sonny's place provided a welcome pause from the constant bombardment on her brain. Her entire body and spirit began to soothe. She felt protected. Katrina appreciated the care he showed her and started to trust him. Her next full day there allowed her to reach a level of normalcy she thought she had lost forever.

In the morning, she approached him and asked if she could call her parents to let them know she was safe. He brought out a satellite phone. It caught her attention. Tracing her call would be difficult. Still, he advised her to make the call brief. Katrina talked to her parents, letting them know she was safe. They seemed unconcerned, as the call was quite cordial and without drama.

The rest of the day was dedicated to lessons, exercises, meditations, healthy eating, and rest. At the end of the day, before turning in, Sonny revealed the plan for the next day. It impressed Katrina, and she felt she was in very capable hands. She slept better than she had in weeks.

The next day started early, filled with traveling and transfers. They packed light, each toting a small carry-on bag. It was a short drive to Monterey Regional Airport. The flight left at about 6 a.m. with a stop in Phoenix. They arrived at Tucson International Airport just before 10 a.m. Exiting the gates, Katrina and Sonny saw "LYLE" on a placard being held by a limo driver. The driver directed them to his vehicle just outside the terminal. He drove them a few miles north to an industrial area and stopped beside a step van waiting in a parking space near a massive warehouse. Transferring to the windowless vehicle, they drove a short distance across railroad tracks, entering a switching yard. The van stopped to let them out, where they were greeted by a woman. Katrina recognized her as one of the students in Sonny's class at Camp Pendleton. The woman introduced herself simply as Wendy.

Wendy led them toward the yard where some of the tracks were empty. After about a quarter mile, they arrived at a lone boxcar on a short, abandoned length of track. Wendy took out a key fob and activated it, causing the center door to slide open and stainless-steel steps to fold out for access.

Katrina turned to look at Sonny and he merely grinned. They entered, Katrina going in first. She immediately recognized it was not a standard boxcar. It was carpeted and elegantly furnished with a polished ebony conference table, black leather chairs, track lighting, a large video screen.

"The yardmaster gets paid nicely by the *Company*," smirked Wendy as she stepped in last.

"The company?" asked Katrina.

"One of the three-letter organizations popularly depicted in spy movies," replied Wendy.

There were two men in the boxcar, sitting at the table. They acknowledged Sonny and Wendy with nods. Both men were wearing ear pieces. Katrina looked around and noticed there were cameras in the ceiling and one across the table. Katrina's intuition gnawed at her. She hated the feeling. No one said a word as Wendy flipped a switch near the door and the steps retracted with the steel door sliding shut. The only thing Katrina could hear was the hum of a generator outside on a platform and the murmur of a condensing unit somewhere above the ceiling.

Once the door shut, the two men got out of their chairs and went to a side wall to pick up identical briefcases. Opening the cases, they took out odd-looking pistols. The guns were made of composites, making them undetectable in transit. Ghost guns. The men proceeded to load a single bullet into the chamber of each gun as Katrina looked on, confused. The condenser above her suddenly stopped working. The four agents looked at each other and nodded. Sonny stepped aside, placing Katrina by herself. Still, no one said a word, and no one sat at the table.

Katrina tried to make eye contact with Sonny. With the door sealed shut, there was no escape. The small windowless interior made her feel claustrophobic. She sensed imminent danger. She realized that no one outside the boxcar knew she was there.

"Please stand with your back against that wall," ordered one of the men.

"What? No! What is happening?" She looked at her companion. "You betrayed me?"

"Do as they say, Katrina," replied Sonny coldly.

Katrina slowly backed to the wall and the lights began to flicker as she wept. The men stood and pointed their weapons at her from the center of the car. In unison, they cocked their hammers. Instantly, the power in the boxcar was gone. The room was in darkness for a brief moment until the emergency power supply activated. As the lights came back on, the men lowered the weapons and uncocked the hammers.

"What happened?" she asked. "What's going on?"

The men went back to the table, took out their rounds, placed the weapons in the cases, closed them, and sat down in their original positions.

"You were the subject of another experiment, Katrina," said Sonny as he positioned himself to sit at the table. "Come here and sit with us. We needed to find a way for you to show your ability, so we could see what you can do."

"There was no way we could have simulated fear. It had to be real," claimed the first man.

What kind of monsters are these people. Who am I dealing with? Katrina thought.

"I know what you're thinking ... you need to realize that back in Grass Valley, you are dealing with people that revel in making people terrified," explained Wendy.

"They either take enjoyment from it, or they just disavow any impact their actions have on people's emotions. It is the essence of a sociopath. It doesn't bother them that they are doing things that could destroy families and lives," said the second man.

"We had anticipated what you would think when we placed you in a terrifying situation. We had hoped it would activate your ability, but we could not anticipate how much. We took that chance," reasoned Sonny.

Wendy walked over to Katrina to look her in the face. "Katrina, we took a risk doing what we did with you to help you, understand?"

Katrina was still standing by the wall where she had been when the two men cocked their pistols. Her clenched fists began to relax. She acknowledged Wendy, then looked at Sonny, slowly nodded, then walked toward the table to sit down. Wendy opened a cabinet to reveal a fine selection of spirits and refreshments, and offered Katrina a drink.

She exhaled, releasing what felt like a huge cloud of fear and stress. "Just cold water is fine for now."

"As I explained, the people doing the energy weapon work on you are part of rogue cell of CIA sponsored scientists and doctors. They are testing psychotronic equipment on you because you revealed you had that ability," said Sonny. "Katrina, we believe those rogue scientists have been using bioelectromagnetic weapons on you. The United States acquired the technology through insiders in the Soviet Union in the seventies. Those people torturing you are brilliant in their work, which is why they were allowed to take the technology and refine it. The program shifted to the nonlethal weaponry office at DARPA, but it appears this cell of scientists have continued on their own."

Katrina voiced her frustration. "So, nobody is going to stop them? Who knows how many other innocent people were tortured so they could learn to improve their toys."

"We can't do anything. CIA would not tolerate internal conflicts that may lead to death," said Wendy.

"But you, Katrina—you are an outsider who is under attack, and you are allowed to defend yourself," added Sonny.

"Fortunately, we just had a hint of what you could do. Can you tell us what other things you can do? What happens when they use the weapon on you?" asked Wendy.

"I seem to have gained more power with every attack in my ability to hear and see things with my mind. My sense in locating people, hearing their thoughts, seeing what they are doing as they project the energy toward me has gotten sharper."

"What you did here, reacting to the threat, is another example of your ability," said Wendy.

"What did I do?" asked Katrina.

"Your mind, perhaps triggered by something like adrenaline or something else, recognized the energy sources and pushed back that energy to its sources. First, you caused the condenser to shut down, then the lights flickered due some short you were causing—possibly the overheating of the wires, then at the end, you shorted the main panel and breaker."

"I did that? Because I was in fear mode? Do I need to be in fear to be able to do that?"

"No, I don't think so," said a male voice, which emanated from the speakers to the side of the video screen.

Wendy activated the video screen and an image appeared of a middle-aged man with black hair, beard, and a mustache, who was sitting behind a desk. "Hello, Katrina. It is nice to finally meet someone on our side with abilities similar to mine. Call me DD. I work with the *Company* when they want me. Right now, I have some free time. You know, I despise the people who use their toys to torture innocent lives. The *Company* doesn't want to deal with them. They don't like complicated relationships. As long as it doesn't pose a threat to the country, they are OK with those rogue units. Katrina, you and I don't need toys to torture people. We have a natural gift. Our minds can do some marvelous things. You see, I have used my mind the way those mad doctors use their expensive and clunky machines. I only use it on those that deserve it, and there are many that deserve it. It's in my family bloodline. I descend from the Borgias . . . old school Mafia. The oldest. There is something to be said about my family line. It may recall some ruthless behavior, but they also passed on a code of honor. Tell me, Katrina, what is important to you right now?"

Without a pause, Katrina responded, "I have a two-year-old daughter, Emma. She is my greatest joy. I look forward to watching her grow up to be a young lady. My older brother died recently from a rare brain cancer. I live at home with my parents to help my mother who has advanced rheumatoid arthritis. Nothing else matters that much right now."

"*La famiglia!* That is the honor handed down from my ancestry. You're a good person, Katrina. You should be helped for the devotion you show to your family, not harmed. I am going to watch over you and help you battle those sadistic bastards, because that is what is happening. You are in a battle. Each day is combat, and so far, they have been in charge, but that is about to change," said DD.

Katrina listened intently for more.

"We are very lucky to have DD. The *Company* recruited him for his ruthless psychological make up," said Wendy. "The rumor is that one of the 'D's stands for *deadly*."

"I wrote *the* manual for assassins. It was a labor of love to devise different ways one can kill a human," the man added with a short cackle.

"True, although he enjoys watching people suffer, it is because he concludes that they deserve it. He may not admit it, but DD can be a sweetheart," assured Wendy.

Is this what needs to happen? Combat? Getting help from an assassin who takes pleasure in watching others suffer? That's some sweetheart. Do I have a choice? Loom wants to kill me. When someone wants to kill, there is no compromise. It's them or me. It's for Mom and Dad and Emma too.

Wendy again reminded Katrina of the kind people with whom she was now dealing. She inhaled deeply. In a perverse way, these people made her feel safe. They understood Katrina and they understood who the threats were. Nobody besides Katrina knew that, and there was nobody else she could rely on for help. She was in an extraordinary predicament. Having a normal life was never her fate. Her father mentioned that. If she were to survive, she needed to change the way she responds to the threats. The safe feeling was a stark difference from the abject terror she had suffered day in and day out in Grass Valley, and the cold rejection by the Russian embassy.

"Katrina, give me some time to figure out how we can get back at those guys," the CIA assassin focused on the mission, his tone even, measured. She appreciated that DD offered a solution. "In the meantime, learn from what happened here today. Fear activated your psychokinetic abilities. Hit back with your mind. You say that when they increase the energy, your senses become sharper. Expand that. Visualize the energy hitting you. Use your mind to reverse it, sending it back to the origin. I will call you in a week to see how you are. You know, I really don't have to call you, I may be able to read you. And when I do, know it's me, and not them, ok?"

Katrina nodded. "Wait, Mr. DD!"

"No Mister, just DD."

"DD, then. Lately, after getting hit with the energy, my spine begins to feel like it's burning. Is there something I can do?" Katrina asked.

"When you know you are going to get hit, fill a tub with water and get plenty of ice. When you start to get the burning sensation, get in, but watch for signs of hypothermia. You should stay in no longer that fifteen minutes."

"I have to do that after every attack?"

"If you do not want to feel the burn, yes."

Silence.

"Anything else?"

"No."

"Alright. That's it for me," DD said. He trained his eyes on his colleagues. "Guys, good job getting Katrina here and setting it up so we could see her reaction. I'm out."

The video screen turned bright blue. The team asked if Katrina had any questions. At that point, she had none. They told her how to contact Sonny if she had any questions. The meeting ended, and Katrina and Sonny returned to California using the same modes of transportation used to arrive in Tucson.

* * *

Emma had to interrupt her mother's story again. "Mom! You were being attacked. No, wait. The rogue scientists in Grass Valley were intent on killing you? And you got help from CIA assassins? All while raising me and caring for Grandma?"

"Pretty crazy, huh? I had no other choice. Grandpa—even he wanted to do something, but he lost contact with people who could have helped, long before I was discovered by Richards."

"I don't care what time it is, I still need something to calm me. How about you, Mom?"

"I am fine, dear. Go ahead. There is so much more."

Emma got up from the couch and went to the kitchen for a glass of wine. She drank some immediately then poured more into her glass before returning to join Katrina.

"Ok, I'm better now. Go ahead, Mom."

* * *

After a brief rest at the studio and some meditation, Katrina drove back to Grass Valley to be with her parents and daughter. When she arrived, she didn't say much about her time away from home, once again because she didn't want to involve her parents more than they were already. Any mention of her ability would add stress to her mother, and her father probably would not approve of her using her mind in combat. They were both innocent, and Katrina preferred they remain that way. Katrina fell asleep, looking forward to testing her abilities against the energy bombardment in the morning.

11

... RETALIATION

As a welcome change, daylight came without anxiety. Katrina likened the sadistic nature of her tormentors to bratty boys who shot BBs at helpless frogs. They were well aware they were causing her pain; they just didn't know how much she could withstand. Just when they guessed she was at her physical limit, Katrina would prove them wrong. They would recalibrate their settings and adjust power to deliver more energy.

The week was more of the same: fifteen-minute sessions on the hour, at an increased level of intensity. When her spine began to feel like it was burning, she drew a bath of cold water. Her sensitivity during the pulses was acute. She read and heard every thought, every conversation clearly. She visualized dull gray painted boxes in a dull gray painted room with fluorescent lights that made everyone look sickly and pale. Was it any wonder these men needed some outside stimulus to make them feel real and to give them a sense of purpose and reason? Every day, for eight hours, someone was assigned to sit on a stool, in a windowless cramped lab, taking notes and working the dials in the most impersonal way, the inhumane acts. It was hard to determine who was under surveillance and confinement—Katrina or the lab technicians.

Her first attack ended exactly on the quarter hour. The scientists, however demented, kept to their own clock discipline. Adherence to their own rules made them predictable, giving Katrina an advantage. She was so amazed by the information *she* collected in the session, she almost forgot about the advice DD gave her about treatment to cool the burning in her spine.

Katrina scampered to fill the tub with cold water, then rushed to the freezer for the ice and dumped them in, trays and all. Four trays of ice were only minimally effective. Cold water from the faucet was cool during spring but not ice-cold, which would be needed for the therapy.

Katrina turned to see her parents' mouths agape, standing in the bathroom doorway. "I know what you're thinking, '*Now, what is she doing?*'" she said, speaking before they could. "The recent bombardment of energy pulses causes my spine to feel like it's on fire. The ice water helps considerably. The temperature of the water cools my neurotransmitters."

Katrina's parents offered no response. This was all too foreign, even for Edwin.

The burning sensation began to subside quickly but not completely. It was enough relief to prevent the more severe reactions of vomiting or doubling over from the pain. She remained in the tub for fifteen minutes. She got out, got dressed, and rushed to the local convenience store for more ice. Katrina stocked the shower stall with ten bags.

Her parents watched her in her frantic mode. She didn't bother to stop and explain the seemingly irrational behavior.

For the remaining days of the week, after each session, she relieved her pain in the same manner. By week's end, Katrina had grown weary of the ice bath routine. She placed a call to her assassin mentor. He was not surprised to get the call.

"I've been expecting you, Katrina," DD said, his tone friendly, welcoming. "I told you I would be monitoring you. Katrina, you are in better control of yourself than most people would be. Those degenerates with their super frequency generators and amplification boxes really have no idea who they are dealing with." DD finished with his signature cackle.

His assessment should have made her feel better, but it didn't. Her world now involved mad scientists and sociopaths, and DD fit so perfectly. She imagined him a super villain turned nice for one citizen—her.

"You could say the same for me," Katrina said, exasperation peeling from her voice.

"You don't give yourself enough credit, and you're too nice for this game. You need to think like them," DD explained. "This world will eat you alive and enjoy hearing you wail while it devours you. They don't bother me because they know about me. They understand I am worse than them. You need to start to thinking like them."

"I think I need to think about what I have become. I want to retaliate." Katrina's response was meant to prove she would follow his advice. "I feel my body fill with hot energy, starting in my head, then flowing down my spine. It's like my mind is a live circuit, overflowing with power, but I'm not sure how to release it. So I keep doing the only thing I know to do, which is to read the enemy deeper. I have learned so much about them. I actually can sense fear as they work on me. It is amazing! The extent of my abilities is unknown to them. That is my advantage. Do you think it is time I fight back?"

"No! Absolutely not! You are not yet in control of your abilities. I still need to have you on training wheels. You are too special to lose."

His comment confused her. "Wait, you just told me to start thinking like them."

"Yes—think. No—don't do. Not now. One misstep on your part could kill you. I believe they are expecting you to retaliate so they can monitor your death. Keeping yourself alive will prolong their anxieties."

Katrina took a deep breath.

"Look, Katrina. I know them because...I was one of them," DD admitted. "The difference this time is that I am on *your* side. Have patience. I am working on something to help you interfere with those frequencies and waves."

Katrina continued to listen to him, realizing her read on him as a super villain was, at its base, correct. Then DD asked about her family. How were they coping with what was happening to her? How was her daughter? He demonstrated great empathy you normally didn't find in a sociopath. She never felt uneasy with him. The phone call ended amicably with Katrina promising not to retaliate. She didn't plan on dying and letting them win.

The following week brought more of the same hectoring and timing with an increase in frequencies and pulses. During the first session, Katrina felt the energy exactly as she had described to DD. She sensed it building inside, from the brain, down her spine, and then her back again. It made her shiver uncontrollably. She felt the buildup in her mind and *saw* the lab clearly in her mind's eye.

Then she heard a familiar voice. Aghast, she recognized it was the voice of one of her physics professors from San Diego State, Dr. Terry Sweet. The staff addressed him as "chief." *Oh my God,* Katrina realized, *the lab is his!* Sweet followed up with off-color comments about Katrina, which caused her to fume, letting something loose inside her. The built-up energy was sent as an explosive burst back to the source. It was a fatal blow, not for Katrina.

Sweet and the victim were equally caught off guard as two of the machines in the laboratory crackled and sparked, then caught fire. The junior researcher, wired to the machines, was violently electrocuted by the surge of energy and killed instantly. Sweet, horrified, hurried to shut down the system. Severe scorch marks crowned the dead man's scalp. The lab smelled of burnt hair and flesh. Sweet set off alarms, signaling base security for help. Unsuspecting lab technicians entered the smoky room and were met by the gruesome sight of a coworker burned alive, their greatest fear realized. One of them had been killed while administering their assault on a subject. The wires on his hands and head piece were fused to what little flesh was left of the partially charred body from the burst of extreme heat.

Sweet tended to the expensive experimental machinery using a halon extinguisher. He looked away from the scene as a cleaning team had come to remove the partially smoldering corpse.

Katrina watched it all through her mind's eye. Even after the release of her own energy, she was still able to sense what was occurring. She had killed a man with her own mind. In the aftermath, her head felt like it had separated from her heavy body. She was exhausted, beyond exhausted, confused and in a fog, trying to piece together the events leading up to the death of the young scientist and the destruction of the lab equipment. The memory of the discussion in the CIA boxcar flashed in her mind. She thought about what DD had said. She needed to convince herself she hadn't done it intentionally. She was coming to the harrowing conclusion that she was being forced to become more like her attackers. Katrina also realized she was far more powerful than anyone could have thought. It troubled her greatly. She reasoned that the lab technician was collateral damage. He just happened to be connected to machines used to torture her. How could she know this wouldn't happen again? She couldn't.

* * *

Emma's eyes were wide with the realization her mother killed another man. "My God, Mom! You killed someone with your mind? Did Grandpa or Grandma know?"

Katrina pursed her lips, and she briefly closed her eyes. "No. They were never told someone died from my actions. I don't think that Grandpa, with all the years in the Navy, ever killed a person. If he knew, I'm sure he would understand, but he probably would have thought differently about me. How about you? Do you think differently of me?"

"After what you were put through? I may be a neonatal nurse, but I know when justice needs to be served. Like you said, you had no choice. They made you, Mom."

Katrina resumed her story.

* * *

Katrina was so tired. She needed to sleep. Surely, the attacks would stop. Would they seek revenge? Would they come after her daughter? Her family? Could anger trigger the same reaction? Could this happen on a road, driving her car, after someone cuts her off? Would a momentary fit of rage manifest into the death of someone else? Katrina realized she needed help. She needed to lie down. She needed to figure out how to either stop this power, or at least control it.

She went to her room and called DD again. "Hello, Katrina. I am still working on a device for you. I need a bit more time."

"DD, I killed someone."

There was no response from her mentor.

Katrina waited for his reaction. When there wasn't one, she added more. "I'm scared. And I'm so tired. I'm exhausted. Whatever happened drained my energy. They were pulsing me just a few minutes ago. I saw everything in my mind. I felt like there was a burst from my mind and a worker that was wired to some machines got electrocuted when my return pulse made the machines explode and spark. I didn't mean to kill him!" Katrina's voice grew to an uncontrollable sob. "I need to lie down."

Finally, DD reacted. It started out as a ... snicker. The snicker built up to a chuckle, then it was followed by an exuberant guffaw.

"Ha! Ha! Ha!" DD cackled. "Woo hoo! YOU ARE STILL ALIVE!?" he shouted boisterously.

The response caught Katrina by surprise, but she understood. He was, after all, a self-proclaimed psychopath, without appreciable conscience or compassion.

"Uh ... yeah, but I feel dead tired."

"And you have no headache ... no pains ... no nausea?"

"Nothing." Her voice trailed off, dragging the last syllable out of her consciousness.

"Unbelievable! Amazing! Do you realize what just happened? You cheated death! You used your mind to send back the energy they were hitting you with, and you walked away without a scratch while the lab was destroyed!"

"And someone died, and I have never felt so tired in my life," Katrina said, horrified by her power, the impact of her power, the fact she just *killed a man. What does that make me?* "I just want to go to bed."

DD suggested she should be ecstatic, given the risks she took. Katrina was tired and weak, and intolerant of DD's cheerful reaction. She was not in the mood.

Finally, he sobered up from his elation and put himself in the role of counselor and mentor to his apprentice. "Katrina, listen. It's not your fault. What you did was a natural reaction to the jolts you were getting. They got what they deserved. Now, they should know better than to pick on you again."

"Don't you think they are going to seek revenge? Could they have me arrested?" Katrina asked.

The CIA assassin let out another cackle, almost losing control at hearing her obvious innocence of how these incidents were handled. He had to stop and pause in order to sound intelligible, but he still managed to chuckle through his response. "Katrina, these are rogue CIA agents doing illegal research. They aren't going to report you to authorities."

Katrina waited until he stopped his chortle. "Well, do you think they might come to my home and do something?" Her fingers strained to keep a grip on the receiver. She almost dropped it. It felt so heavy, so unnatural against her skin.

"No. They are geeks with toys. They are cowards. That's why they hide in their lab all day."

How could he hold such a low opinion of these men who have been torturing me, trying to slowly drive me to my death? Katrina wondered.

"They only work in the manner that you have been subjected to. They may try more torture, perhaps a different kind, even try to kill you with their boxes, but they won't come to your house. They don't work like that."

"I still don't understand what happened and why. You know what is happening to me. I don't want to kill anyone again." Katrina practically begged her assassin friend, who prided himself in executions, to help her not to kill again.

DD made an effort to reason with her before she went off the rails. "Too late. It happened because *they* caused it. They were experimenting. They knew the risks. They knew exactly what they were doing to you. If they do it again, your brain and its psychokinetic ability will defend you."

"What? psycho...," she yawned.

"Psychokinetic. your brain has the ability to project energy. You also have the ability to remote view. You can see activity with your mind's eye. Distance is irrelevant in certain energy spectrums. They recognize that you have those abilities and they want to replicate them with their machines. They need wires, and generators, and amplifiers. You don't need any of that, and still your power is greater. Instead of you being afraid, they are the ones that should be afraid, and I'll bet they are. Katrina, don't...be...afraid! Lose that fear! You are an amazing part of creation. Be proud, but use your gift wisely, not like them."

"What if they decide to attack me with more power?"

"I don't think they are stupid enough to try that, but if they do, they deserve whatever your brain decides to do to fight back. Technically, all you did was use their energy in the electromagnetic spectrum they applied to you. When your brain reached its storage limit, you released it. All the pulses were absorbed and stored until it could do so no longer and then, in one jolt, it blasted its way back to the source of the energy. Essentially, *they* killed that man. This will only happen if your mind senses energy, absorbs it, and releases it back to any source. That is what happened in Tucson. The fear was part of an energy wave in your mind, brought out by a catalyst like adrenaline, and you reversed the energies you sensed to the sources."

Katrina let the phone drop out of her hand as her head nodded. The thump on the floor startled her awake. DD sensed what was happening. She picked up the phone again. The weight of the receiver surprised her.

"Katrina, you need to get rest now. You won't be able to function well for a while," DD said, his level of basic compassion again surprising her. "Your brain not only sent their energy back, it used some your own energy as part of the response. Call me when you wake up if you want."

"Ok, thanks for your help."

"Are you still scared? I'll keep an eye on you."

"No ... wait ... how are you going to do that?"

"I have abilities too, Katrina, similar, but not as potent as yours. Now go to bed."

Katrina ended the call with a "good night," although it was mid-morning. Her mentor hung up and resumed work on the device for her.

She mustered enough energy to stumble from her room. She looked at her parents with a vacant gaze and told them she needed to lie down. Finally, she collapsed face down on the bed and did not move until the next day.

That following morning, her parents, worried that they had not seen nor heard their daughter since before noon the day before, knocked on the door. After they didn't receive a response, they opened the door to find her on the bed in her clothes, sprawled, face down. Her mother went to check her pulse. It was faint.

She tried to wake her daughter. Katrina was groggy, hardly able to lift her head. Her parents suspected her behavior was in response to whatever the town's scientists were doing to her. Her father was more aware of the details than her mother. He kept those details to himself, and her mother did not press the issue. Hermann assured his wife that Katrina would be fine if they left her alone to get more sleep. Meanwhile, she left her bed only to use the bathroom.

On the third morning, she finally felt alive enough to leave the horizontal position. The first thing she did was call DD again.

"Hi. It's Katrina."

"I know what you are going to tell me, Katrina. You just woke up from a hard sleep. Yes. You could have died."

"What?" DD's terse statement jerked Katrina out of her fog of dormancy.

"I was monitoring you. I checked your brain activity. I used psychokinetics while you slept to heal you. It is like Reiki healing but more direct and using a different energy frequency. You had some nerve damage, and you may have short term memory loss, but you are alive. Try not to do that again until I get my device to you."

"But I told you I had pressure building. It was instinctive."

"Well, now you understand the risks." This time, DD was stern with her. "Don't do anything until I am finished with this device. Is that clear?"

"What *are* you working on?"

"Something that will keep you alive during your energy releases."

He asked her again how she was feeling. "Somewhat rested," she said, "no pain, no dizziness."

He was impressed; he expected her to be woozy and shaken. Katrina assured him that she would be more careful if it happened again.

"Just remember there are other labs in the circuit, and more torture could come your way sooner than expected," he said, sternly warning her. "If they return to hurt you, they will have to deal with me, either directly or indirectly. I don't need their expensive contraptions to inflict pain. As I told you, I'm not like you. In a perverse way, I *want* them to attempt to harm you. It's been a while since I had the satisfaction of applying my own psychokinetics on a deserving scoundrel. Humans have such creative ways to express pain. It's fascinating to watch a body contort uncontrollably. It's not really a pleasure—more of an observation as a scientist. They do the same when they work on you."

Listening to DD describe his enthusiasm for torture made Katrina shudder. This monster, who was a monster to everyone except her and his work colleagues, was her strongest ally, and she needed him now, more than ever. Every time she considered the inhumane nature of her mentor, and accepting his sadistic nature, she imagined another part of her younger, cheerful, innocent self, sublimate into the air.

"Are you still there? I get nostalgic about those days and then I daydream aloud. I hope I didn't put you back to sleep."

"No...no...I...was temporarily distracted by something outside my window," she lied.

"I'll call you when I'm ready to ship the device," DD said. The call ended with DD strongly advising her to wait before retaliating.

Katrina looked at the phone in the base unit, still with one hand on it, then she let go, leaving her hand within touch of the base. The conversation elevated her to a new reality. There was no going to back to who she had been. She had to accept the fact that she destroyed a lab and killed a man. She possessed a power to do things with her mind, but she had no control over it. Evil people with bad intentions knew that. Her abilities made her a prize, a trophy. She wondered if this made her less human. She came to grips with the somber realization that her life depended upon a fiendish man who relished handing out torture to deserving "hunters."

And what about her? Had she gone crazy? Considering all the people she had met recently, she surmised that not one of them was perfectly sane. There was no such thing as a perfect brain, so everyone—*everyone* had some form of mental illness, however subtle. People talk to themselves. People have phobias. People behave irrationally, often enough. She may no longer be sane, but rationalizing that no one else was made it easier to accept the situation she was in.

It didn't take long for the harassment to return. The intensity did not seem to increase, but she could tell that the signals were coming from a different source. It started out the first morning as a low frequency drone, much like the beginning. The hum was so subtle, it extended virtually no impact to her daily life. It was a welcome awareness. As the day passed, the intensity increased ever so slightly. By day's end she suffered no deleterious side effects. *No burning? No dizziness? Awesome.*

She wondered if her mentor healer had interceded, minimizing what was administered. She decided to call him one more time. "Yes, Katrina. I am still working on your device. I am almost done," DD said.

Katrina explained the harassment had little-to-no effect on her. She felt the energy spectrum increase, and her senses sharpened, but there was no side effect. "While I was asleep and you healed my brain, did you do something to prevent me from feeling the energy pulses?" she asked.

"I suppose it's possible," DD said, intrigued by her question, certain he had not done anything beyond keeping her brain from deterioration. There should not have been any physiological change that would allow her brain to defend itself from the effects of the pulses.

Katrina was confused and disappointed with his response. Their call ended with both parties questioning how much they understood of Katrina's abilities.

The following day, the scientists pulsed her with greater intensity, which allowed her to envision the perpetrators and the new location. This time, the signals were originating from Sweet's private lab at San Diego State, and there appeared to be a network of labs connected in this experiment through a satellite link at Beale Air Force Base. The labs were located in a building that shared space with an intelligence unit. The room with the surveillance equipment featured metal lockers with perforated steel panels. Each locker held a tagged item and was secured with a padlock. Next to the lockers, in the cramped room, was an electronic cabinet and panels with blinking, colored lights. A young airman was monitoring the system. Everything was unmistakably clear.

As the week continued, the energy pulses grew stronger. As they intensified, her headaches re-emerged. With each passing hour, the pain became stronger, and she once again felt the buildup in her mind. Again, her brain felt like a war of the hemispheres. Throbbing pain volleyed from left hemisphere to right. The buildup of energy in her brain created unbearable pressure. She felt it travel throughout her body, running down her spine like molten lava. Her spine started to tingle. The tingle phased into a buzz.

Anxiety engulfed her. Would she explode if she didn't release the energy? DD told her explicitly not to release until she received his device. Now her spine began to burn. She couldn't hold it back any longer. She was at her limit, and she knew she held the power to stop the assault. She had the labs in her sights.

The breaking point hit. She thrust the energy back to the source in one massive bolt.

Sweet sat in his lab, monitoring the new equipment he and his crew had spent months building, testing, rebuilding, and retesting. A slight crackle began behind the casework, then sharp pops flared up and down the cabinet. Sweet grew flush, his mouth flying open as smoke appeared from the bottom of the cabinet front, wafting through the lab. He smelled the distinctive odor of burning wires and insulation.

Panic swept through him. He pushed the shunt to cut power, but it was too late. The equipment quickly caught fire. Alarms sounded. Sweet reached for the halon bottle, but the fire grew too hot too quickly. It spread to papers strewn on an adjacent desk. The back wall began smoldering.

Just in time, a colleague came to his aid with the correct type of extinguisher and put the flames out. The acrid smoke from the burning plastic and components lingered in the room like the aftermath of a gun battle. Almost a billion dollars' worth of high-technology experimental equipment, carefully crafted from the finest components through many long nights, was destroyed in seconds.

***

At the Beale Air Force Base security building, an airman was caught by surprise as the equipment arced and the room became a fireworks show, igniting combustible evidence in the lockers. He rushed for an extinguisher down the hall, only to return to fires in the lockers and a smoking tower of equipment he had been assigned to monitor. He put the fire out before it blazed out of control. The materials in the lockers, evidence from crimes under investigation, was damaged beyond further use.

Katrina felt the release sap her own energy. She collapsed in her room, passing out. Her parents found her the next morning, on the floor. She had vomited. Her alarmed mother could only weep as Katrina remained in a dream state. Her father treated the situation as though he were dealing with a fallen soldier in wartime, tending to her without emotion, his brain rapidly assessing the situation. He woke her.

The phone rang in the background. It stopped, and she could hear her mother's voice. Opening her eyes, with her head turned and against the floor, she smelled the putrid, rank scent of vomit against her face and neck. Looking at her father kneeling over her, she slowly raised her head. The room was spinning. Shifting her upper body away from the mess, she turned over, and shut her eyes. Her mother entered the room and told her a man who called himself Dee Dee was on the phone.

Katrina took the phone, remaining horizontal on the floor. "Hello?" she asked in a groggy stupor, wiping her mouth.

"You did it again, didn't you?"

"I . . . what time is it?"

Her mother brought her a cool wet facecloth to wipe herself. She held the towelette to her forehead.

"I should say good morning, Katrina, how does it feel to destroy the work of a dedicated scientist's life ambition?"

Almost in a whisper, Katrina begrudgingly replied, "I couldn't stop it from happening. I was scared. The pressure felt like my body was going to explode. I couldn't handle the pain from the burning in my spine. I figured, if I die, I was taking them with me."

"And?"

"And what?"

"How do you feel now?"

"The worst hangover you could ever imagine. I'm tired. I can't get off the floor."

"I am asking you like a doctor now, so I need a thorough and truthful response. What happened immediately after you hit them with your energy?"

"I don't know. I lost consciousness. I guess I fainted."

"You know, I felt the release here in Illinois, and I cursed, realizing that you had done it again. It should have damaged you, but I detected nothing wrong with your third eye chakra."

"I got sick. It's a good thing I landed face down, or I would have suffocated."

"You didn't faint or throw up the last time this happened, did you?"

"No."

"Are you in any pain right now?"

"I have a doozy of a headache." After responding, she held the phone away from her ear to abate the volume of his voice.

"Are you dizzy?"

"Yes, I am still a bit dizzy and a little sick."

Katrina's mother came in to clean the floor, and Katrina obliged by shifting her upper body slightly again.

"It sounds like the effects on you were greater this time, and yet …I am reading your third eye chakra." DD paused. "Amazing! I don't detect anything out of order or imbalance. You sent out an enormous amount of energy to do what you did … which means you were taking in a lot of electromagnetic energy … and you're still alive."

Katrina blinked once, then again. "What are you getting at?"

"You are not a common psy phenom; you are unique. Special. Your brain is not only repairing itself after these attacks, it seems to be making you more resilient and powerful. I'll bet they are scared now. They truly do not know what your limit is, and they don't know how powerful your ability is. I don't think they have equipment powerful enough to affect you. I am still recommending the device I am sending you tomorrow. You should get it in a couple days. I will provide instructions. Listen, just in case they intend on hitting you with more, don't do anything until you get the device. I think I mentioned this to you before."

"Yes, I know. Thank you."

While she was on the phone, her mother quickly cleaned the carpet. Katrina, still sick, still dizzy, still tired, turned over to her original position and closed her eyes. She needed another night of rest.

The few days that followed were without incident, but Katrina wasn't quite ready to claim victory. The absence of any pulses, hums, vibrations, seemed almost out of place and irregular. She had come to accept some sort of harassment or torture as part of her day-to-day routine.

Then the continuum of the few days of silence was halted by a delivery. It was DD's device. Katrina inspected the contents and discovered it was nothing she had imagined. A handwritten note read:

> *"Katrina. This is a modified Faraday enclosure. It is designed to shield you from electromagnetic pulse attacks. I used heavy cardboard to make it lighter for you than wood. Have someone help you position it so you are enclosed at the top and sides. The copper wire mesh should be on the inside. I am working on something more effective and portable, and I hope to get it to you soon."*

Katrina kept it in her room where she would be able to retrieve it quickly. The rest of the day was quiet, spending time with her parents and her daughter. Katrina felt uneasy with the lull in activity. She went to bed, waking up often in anticipation of action.

* * *

At dawn, the entire household was thrust into an escalation of combat unlike anything they'd yet experienced. A sonic boom shook the entire house. Windows rattled like a mid-level seismic event. Anything with a printed circuit board was destroyed in an instant. Unknown to the Hermanns, their house became ground zero for a precise electromagnetic pulse (EMP) event. The blast frightened her mother and daughter out of bed. Her father was more upset than scared. Katrina couldn't help think this was retaliation for the fire and that she was putting her family in harm's way. The reaction from her mother and child, and the destruction to her parents' possessions and property, touched off an anger she had never known before.

No longer was she afraid. She had cheated death twice and had withstood torture for weeks. She had earned a sense of invincibility from the scientists' failed attempts. Was this demonstration meant to intimidate her? The intimidation game was over. She understood now what she was, what she could do ... what she had to do in spite of DD's advice. There was no more coming back from the madness in the labs.

For the rest of the day, Katrina and her parents switched to high alert, anxiously awaiting the next "message." There was no more activity. They did not immediately replace any of the damaged electronic devices. She did go to retrieve her PC and press the switch to turn it on. Nothing. Not even an error message.

Katrina's father walked to the carport to check on the cars. Both started. Evidently, the blast was more direct and focused on the house and Katrina. Her PC was critical, so she took it to a repair shop in Sacramento. The technician opened the case, and an expression of wonder crossed his faced. He found damage...a very specific kind of damage. "Do you live between two super magnets?" he asked. "Damage like this could only be done from that. It's beyond salvage."

12

... PSYCHIC AFFAIRS

The effects of the last attack were felt by everyone in the house. Edwin was visibly disturbed by the blatant act escalating the conflict, hurting the entire family. It was an undertaking distinctly more violent than anything he had anticipated by the CIA scientists. He was certain the *Company* would not have condoned such an attack. Pragmatically speaking, the ratio of cost of operation to target alone was prohibitive. Equipment worth millions of dollars used to destroy a TV, appliances, and a computer? It made no sense.

Katrina's mother was silent about the event. Saying anything was beyond her level of assumed authority. She always trusted Edwin on matters pertaining to outside threats. However, on this occasion, she detected an uneasiness in his reaction, and it troubled her. Just as his wife regarded his handling of such an affair with trust, Edwin placed his confidence in Katrina's management of the situation. Katrina was also noticeably agitated. The family's lack of communication worked against them. No one spoke of the incident. The silence compounded the uneasiness. Even the recent cataclysm of electromagnetic energy would not work to prompt a change in the way they related to each other.

The days following the EMP event remained relatively quiet in activity and conversation. Katrina and her family used the lull in activity to repair or replace electronics. They replaced the home telephone and computer first. Appliances without circuit boards had survived.

Not long after the phones were replaced, Katrina received a call from Sonny in Monterey. She was pleasantly surprised and took comfort in hearing his voice and the usually grounded language he chose. He informed her of a psychic fair happening at San Diego

State, her alma mater, the coming weekend. He urged her to meet people with similar abilities and to make connections. "Will you be attending?" Katrina asked, wishing and hoping he would.

"I might, but I won't be staying long."

After giving her information on registering and contacts, they ended the call. Her spirit was lifted by the thought of going to the fair.

Katrina desperately wanted to be understood. She yearned to find someone besides DD who was familiar with psychokinetics. She wished she could find someone to confide in who was not a sociopath, someone with similar abilities. Once she arrived, she used her familiarity with the campus to make her way quickly to the College's Center, which functioned as the exhibit hall. The event covered many topics related to psychic phenomena. Following a printed diagram, she navigated the labyrinth of signs, counters, partitions, and other barriers. In her search, she passed by booths for Reiki healers, Tarot card readers, remote viewers, incense dealers, paranormal book authors, meditation coaches, and new age musicians.

Finally, in a darker corner away from the main aisle, next to a fire exit, she found the austere booth for psychokinesis information. Approaching her destination, she caught sight of the person behind the counter, and he recognized her immediately.

"Ms. Hermann!" Doctor Sweet bellowed.

"Doctor Sweet. Of course. I should have realized you would be here. Doing some recruiting of unsuspecting innocent youth?"

What might have been an awkward meeting for Katrina quickly escalated to a challenge of confidence and courage. Sweet was less than pleasant, often capturing the attention of by-standers with his condescending direct tone.

"I suppose you are quite proud of yourself, Katrina," he said.

Katrina moved closer to him so she could keep her voice down. "You gave me little choice. I was sensing my natural reaction under extreme stress, and I followed through with my instinct."

"Instinct?" He walked even closer to her, lowering his voice so only she would be able to hear. "You killed a man!" He stepped back. "You have no control over your own abilities! You are a threat to yourself and society. The extent of your abilities is unknown to us. Science must be served regardless of the costs. You are a risk, and to have you roam around freely is not in the best interest of those around you. You are a misfit: a mutant." Sweet annunciated the words sharply and slowly to chide Katrina. "There is a bomb inside you, and nobody, not even you, knows how powerful it is or when it may strike. You must be stopped."

"I use only what I have as a defense. Instead of attacking me, you should be helping me understand what I have," she replied having no problem responding to his insults.

He whispered closely to her, but it was loud enough for someone nearby to hear the accusation. "In a perverse way, we are. You are learning about yourself, just as we are."

"It was unintentional," Katrina reiterated. "How do you think I feel about it? I am not the one administering torture just to see how much a person can take!"

She glanced to her right to notice a young woman overhearing the conversation. Katrina stepped outside her benign self. "Do you mind? This is a private matter! You see this booth? It's about an ability to manipulate our world with the mind. Unless you leave, I may have to show you an example, and you may not like the results."

The woman quickly turned and walked briskly away to another part of the exhibition.

Katrina turned back to face Sweet, who pointed his finger at her chest. "Do you realize that you also damaged close to a billion dollars' worth of advanced experimental equipment—one-of-a-kind projects put together by brilliant scientists?"

"Do you realize none of that equipment would have been damaged if you hadn't used it on me?" Katrina retorted. "Why are you torturing me and now my family? What did you use to damage our electronics?"

"Oh, it's just something we got out of storage, dusted it off, did some modifications. It is nothing compared to what is coming, Katrina."

"What makes you think that I will not be able to defend myself again? Are you really willing to take that chance? How do you know I won't accidentally kill others—maybe even you, Doctor?"

"This is uncharted territory for both sides, Katrina. You have no idea of the resources we have, should you retaliate—accidentally or intentionally."

"You better look at your risks again, doctor. I have my own team behind me, and they are not as nice and innocent as I seem to be."

Katrina turned and left the show, no longer in any mood to view exhibits or make contacts. She was beginning to view her ability as a curse instead of a gift, and would wish it away if she could.

***

For a while, all was quiet after the EMP attack. Then came a knock on the door. Looking out the window, Katrina saw a man in an Air Force pilot's flight suit. She opened the door just enough for him to see her, and he introduced himself as Major Kyle Upshaw, a U-2 pilot stationed at Beale Air Force Base. She glanced back at her father. Meeting her eyes, he nodded, motioning to her to let the pilot in. Katrina was caught by surprise, not knowing what the visit was about.

"Come in, Major. You came a bit sooner than I anticipated. Nevertheless, come sit down," Edwin said, waving his hand.

The retired Navy intelligence officer had pulled some old strings to get help from people he could trust. His contact in the Pentagon directed him to the major because the officer professed an interest in psychokinetics. After ushering everyone into the living room, the Navy retiree introduced Katrina and the rest of the family. Major Upshaw smiled at Katrina then explained the reason for his visit. He confided it was not an official government visit. He was curious about her and her abilities. Her father assured Katrina that she could trust the major. Katrina, in turn, explained everything that had happened to her from the time she discovered her abilities when her brother passed, to the most recent retaliation on Doctor Sweet's lab. Major Upshaw asked probing questions regarding her sanity, perhaps at her father's request. After a third effort to talk about her mental health, Katrina uncharacteristically retorted.

"Major, what gives you the impression that I am not of a stable mind? Just because I am different from you doesn't classify me as insane by your standards. I said by your standards, because how do you know you are completely sane?"

Not by coincidence, her emotional rebuke was accompanied by a flicker of the lights in the house. The event startled everyone as the major looked around the room, witnessing Katrina's ability. He was self-conscious about his approach. Katrina's reaction was without emotion. She was learning to step into the sociopath's role.

"I can understand why you are being targeted. Did you mean to do that?" asked the major in a serious tone.

Katrina stared at him with no change in her expression. Her demeanor unnerved the Air Force pilot. For the first time he encountered a threat with unknown weaponry and capability. Her father stepped in to defuse the situation. "Katrina, the major has been kind enough to come, at my request, to help you."

"Insulting me doesn't help, Dad. I know quite well what I have and what my problem is. Major, you only have a hint of what I have been through. Anyone else in my position would have either crumbled and surrendered, or obliterated those masochists. Fortunately, for others, I still have my senses and my conscience is still strong."

"Katrina, Major Upshaw is interested in your ability. He has also offered to introduce you to other officers on the base. It's an opportunity to once again enjoy a social life and not be affected by the scientists in town."

Major Kyle Upshaw looked at Katrina sincerely and nodded in agreement with her father. Katrina refrained from further defensive words.

The pilot then apologized to Katrina. He rose from the chair, announcing he should be getting back to the base, then took out a business card and offered it to Katrina, inviting her to the Officers' Club to meet other pilots from his squadron. She accepted the apology, the card, and the invitation. Edwin thanked Upshaw for taking the time to visit. The major left with a courteous salute.

Major Upshaw called later in the week. He kept his promise and arranged for her to go the Officers' Club, where there was a squadron gathering and a presentation on a weapon system in development. Upshaw let her know that he was scheduled to fly the next day to Langley Air Force Base, Virginia. He would be gone only for a couple days and then return in time for the presentation. He told her he hoped to see her at the Club. Katrina was intrigued about meeting other men in uniform.

Katrina began to experience another, more passive ability with her mind. She was easily able to remote view, that is, use her mind to see activity anywhere she felt a need to see. The next evening, she picked up Upshaw's business card, and while thinking about him, saw him at Langley's Officers' Club, in the bar, sitting and talking to a younger woman. Katrina dropped the card, and the vision disappeared. The sight of him with another woman skewered her impression of him. Upshaw was married. She saw the ring on his finger as she sat across from him during his visit.

She decided to take her mind away from her discovery. Perhaps he was just there to talk and socialize. Nothing wrong with that. She went to watch TV with her parents. Afterward, she returned to her room and picked up the business card again. Another revealing vision appeared. Upshaw wasn't at the Club anymore. He was at the Visiting Officers' Quarters, and he wasn't alone. Katrina cut her connection. Only now, did she realize another part of her ability. Physical barriers had no impact on her. It was evident she was a genuine, walking security risk.

* * *

The day of the event at the Officers' Club, Upshaw and his wife arrived to pick Katrina up. Katrina was quiet, still unable to set aside the visions she had of the major at his lodging room while he was away. Casually, Kyle Upshaw mentioned Katrina's abilities to his wife.

"Katrina, I told Carrie you are psychic."

Katrina bit her lip, stifling any urge to expose his infidelities.

"Oh, Katrina, I hope you demonstrate that for me some time," Carrie Upshaw said. "I would love to know more about the world around me. I tend to be isolated when Kyle goes on temporary duty. The other officers' wives are the same. They gossip, they wear their husbands' rank, or they have catalog merchandise parties and "housewife" presentations. I have never been comfortable anywhere with those women. It is wonderful to know someone on the outside."

Great! Katrina thought. *She is genuine, so I feel sorry for her even more.*

"That makes two of us, Carrie. I didn't have friends in school, and I have lost contact with my 'Navy brat' friends. We moved a lot, and some places were in sparsely populated areas. Plus, the other parents thought my dad was strange, and that carried down to me." The memory of being an outcast due to her father's work remained an open wound.

After a half hour of driving through the rural arid California landscape, the car approached the gate at Beale. It took another fifteen minutes to get to the Club. Once inside, Katrina sat with Kyle, Carrie, and three more couples at a large round table seating ten. The ballroom was starkly furnished with office-style lighting, and a well-worn, monotonous interior. It showed the financial effect of operations, maintenance, and construction not being funded by taxpayers, by law. The money came from the base personnel support of all NAF activities on the base, and spending was severely scrutinized.

The presentation, delivered by the Air Force Association, concerned Aurora, a high velocity, high altitude reconnaissance aircraft that would replace the SR-71 Blackbird. The audience was happy to hear that the U-2 would continue to be used for tactical reconnaissance. Conversation was cordial, civil, at times jovial. And delightfully stress-free, a welcome departure from the negativity that stalked her when she was home. Katrina was even introduced by the major to some single U-2 pilots. Before the evening ended, with the help of a little "liquid courage," Katrina exchanged phone numbers with a few of the young officers.

Carrie, however, no longer seemed her cheerful and talkative self. Katrina walked to the table to sit down next to her. Katrina couldn't read her mind; that was not a part of her repertoire as a psychic.

"Are you alright, Carrie?"

Mrs. Upshaw's eyes looked up at Katrina. "I need to talk to you about something that has been bothering me, but not here, not tonight."

Carrie reached in her purse to get her phone and asked Katrina for her number. She told her she would call tomorrow when Kyle was at the squadron's headquarters. Katrina didn't need to be a mind reader to know what Carrie was talking about. It weighed on her mind and tempered the giddy feelings she felt while talking to the pilots who only identified themselves by their call signs: Pony, Pump, Judge, Mod, and although she knew him as Kyle, his patch read "Twaddler."

After a few more rounds at the bar, exactly at midnight, the lights turned bright to signal the end of the night. Carrie drove them home, with Katrina in the front seat and Kyle laid across the seat in the back, more tired than inebriated.

The next morning, as promised, Carrie called Katrina. She let Carrie talk while she listened. Then Carrie asked her about her abilities and Katrina replied honestly and accurately.

"After I found out from Kyle, about your ability, thoughts entered my mind," Carrie said.

Silence.

Carrie resumed talking. "Kyle tried to explain remote viewing to me, but I just couldn't get past the psychic thing in the first place. He said you can see images from anywhere if you focus on the subject."

"Well, until recently, I was only able to do it if someone was to send me an electromagnetic pulse. Once I got the pulse, I was able to get to the source and view activity. I have only been able to see things without that stimulus recently."

"Can I give you a test?"

Hesitatingly, Katrina replied, "Sure, okay."

"Okay. Can you see me?"

"Yes."

"What am I wearing now?"

"You are wearing pink sweatpants and a Niners sweatshirt."

After a pause, Carrie asked her next question: "Is he sleeping with someone?"

Silence.

Carrie understood the silence but stressed her point. "Hello? Katrina, are you still there?"

"Yes, I heard you. What made you ask that question?"

Carrie explained that she would catch Kyle texting and appearing to be secretive. She also mentioned that other pilots' wives accidentally revealed the gossip, thinking she was not able to hear. The wives would get word from their husbands. "What is it with pilots?" she asked rhetorically.

Katrina, still feeling uncomfortable about adding validity to the gossip, let Carrie finish answering her own question. Carrie began to sob. "The stories are true, I guess."

After another uncomfortable silence, Carrie spoke again, now reduced to a plea. "Katrina, you seem to be the most genuine person I know. I don't trust anyone here on the base, including Kyle, now. I need a friend that I can talk to without thinking it would be used against me. Will you meet us at the chapel Sunday and sit with me?"

Katrina agreed to go to church services the following Sunday with Carrie. She thanked Katrina and ended the call.

Katrina's ability continued to grow stronger. The lack of control over what was happening to her made her recall the incident that resulted in the death of a young scientist. In that case, her inability to control her energy release proved lethal. She cringed at the thought. She couldn't keep it out of her mind.

Then her Sunday morning at the Protestant base chapel brought an unsettling event. During the service, she saw in her mind's eye the image of a scene high over a foreign barren landscape. She was somehow *connected* to the camera equipment and could see that the target of reconnaissance was a compound of bunker-like structures. She did not know where it was, nor the pilot or plane. She guessed it was one of the U-2s. She noticed the sun was low over the western horizon, which meant it was not in the US, since it was early morning in California. When the pilot shut down the camera equipment, Katrina's visions disappeared.

Both Carrie and Kyle noticed that Katrina seemed as if her thoughts were miles away. Carrie's efforts to communicate with Katrina were hampered by Katrina's distracted mind. She would not tell Carrie, and certainly not Kyle, about her vision of a possibly classified recon mission in a land far away. Carrie invited her to brunch at the Officers' Club, but Katrina requested a rain check, saying she was feeling out of sorts and needed to get rest.

The next day, Katrina was presented again with a most incredible series of experiences from her ability to remote view. As with the previous remote view, she did not initiate the activity. It appeared as a headache appears—without warning, out of nowhere. Katrina saw another image similar to the one in church. It appeared to be over another military installation. She noticed solar collectors, exotic looking craft, and facilities painted in a dark color. An opening in the ground appeared, where an exotic vehicle was entering. Just when she was able to see detail, the vision disappeared, likely a result of the pilot shutting down the camera equipment. She did not reveal these psychic events to anyone. Only if she was in close proximity to Beale, and there was a U-2 reconnaissance mission or training at the same time, would she get the image that the camera equipment was transmitting.

She continued to stay in touch with Carrie and Kyle while they were still stationed at Beale. But as she grew increasingly wary about being exposed to the reconnaissance and training missions, she made excuses not to visit. What other things would her ability allow her do? She was unnerved by the notion that the remote view activity was not at her command. And she knew Kyle did not change his philandering ways. Eventually, someone, a righteous pilot or a jealous partner, reported his antics to the Squadron Commander. Infidelity was considered a security risk. Kyle and his extracurricular activities were grounded, and it actually brought relief to both Katrina and Carrie. Kyle and Carrie were later transferred to the Program Office at Aeronautical Systems Division, Wright-Patterson Air Force Base, Ohio.

13

. . . TURNING UP THE HEAT

DD devised another gadget that was more effective and practical than the Faraday cage. He called it the *Hermann Biocircuit*. It was nothing more than a box with circuitry composed of resistors, capacitors, and copper mesh. There was no ON button, no power cord, and batteries were not required. He assured her in his note that it would work better than the enclosure he had sent previously. It reduced the risk of damage to Katrina's brain. This invention would also ensure her own energy would not be exhausted and compromised to a deadly level. Katrina placed the biocircuit in her room, next to her bed, took apart the enclosure, and put it away in a closet, never to be used again.

The following week started with another barrage of electromagnetic attacks. Her abilities, combined with the new biocircuit, made her a powerful foe. Her attackers were under-energized, undermanned, and unprepared for what happened once she sensed the activity. It wasn't torture anymore; it was mild harassment, and, following DD's advice, she was through being nice. DD had never been treated in the manner she had because he was ruthless. He had no regrets about collateral damage, so no one attacked him. Having the reputation of a madman proved an effective deterrent.

Now Katrina was tired of the harassment. It made her intent on following her mentor's example. During one particular attack, she saw one of the scientists at his machine. Looking around the office adjacent to the lab, she noticed a fancy, well-stocked aquarium with an assortment of exotic tropical fish. As she focused on the aquarium, she sensed the water temperature rising. In a heartless fashion, she monitored the increase, which rendered the aquarium a fatal bath for the fish. None of the specimens survived.

Katrina viewed her work. She had no intention of having it affect her emotionally. She passed that test, surprising herself. She carried out the dastardly task without hesitation. She had crossed the line too easily.

It was close to the end of the day for the scientist. He shut down the equipment, got up from his chair, and walked toward the door, switching off the light. Entering his suite, horror washed over his face as he walked toward the tank that kept his aquatic collection safe and clean. Cautiously, he approached the tank, extending his hand toward the glass, feeling an unusually high level of heat. Stopping short of touching the tank's surface, he stood in shock, understanding that the temperature rise was from Katrina's brain activity. The dejected scientist rued the day he agreed to take part in the research that developed into a series of torture sessions on the mysterious woman. This event caused him to resign from the project.

Perhaps it was their motivation as scientists, feeling the need to continue experimentation regardless of the ethics. Perhaps it was a male ego response to a strong woman, thinking they could break her. Whatever the reason, the scientists did not know it, but their continuous harassment, torture, and the unprovoked attacks affecting her family pushed Katrina to her limit. Even she was surprised by her own retaliation. Once she crossed over that line separating caution and sanity from the reckless release of an unquantifiable, powerful force, it was easier to feel less human: to feel less in general. Risks did not figure into her decisions anymore. Being something beyond human meant having less in common with the men that attacked her. She never could have imagined becoming such a person only months ago. Putting the blame on her attackers made it easy. Listening to the sociopath who watched over her made it easier. Wanting to be a force and dispense with being a victim made it deliciously easy.

Even with the protection of the biocircuit, Katrina was left exhausted after each attack. She called DD and told him she was done. She wanted the harassment to end. She told him of her exhaustion, even with the biocircuit in her possession. She was exasperated and tired of being held hostage to the scientists' whims.

"DD, I'm telling you, I can't take anymore. The next time they try to hijack my brain, I will make sure it is their last time." She added she was willing to die if it would give her peace.

"They think that they have a right to torture you 'in the name of science.' To them, you are a project, not a human with feelings.

Using numbers to study you further dehumanizes you. They are not conditioned to care about your feelings. I, however, thrive on understanding the feelings of my subjects. Katrina, you do what you feel you have to do. I cannot stop you. But if you are going to succeed, you must think like me. You have to want to take pleasure in returning the pain they send to you. As for me, I will watch you again, and if they *do* decide to escalate these battles, not only will they suffer your wrath, they will also have to deal with me."

"What are you planning to do?"

"I am going to pay the lead scientist in Grass Valley, Loom, a visit."

"Are you going to travel all the way here to California for me?"

"I don't need to physically travel. He will know it when I visit him."

Katrina thanked him for his support. Sensing despair in her voice, DD assured her that everything would turn out fine. He chuckled as they said goodbye to each other, wishing he could have been in her place to return the fire.

The following week, Katrina was awakened by another dose of harassment and pain. It was more acute. She reached for her biocircuit and held it against her body. The pain was reduced significantly, to a dull ache. She was able to view a new facility in the network: the Rancho Seco nuclear power plant southeast of Sacramento. One of the scientists in the network was working from a secure office in a remote part of the facility. The change in facility and equipment explained the change in power she felt. She saw familiar faces in other separate offices in the network.

She quickly recognized a way to end this conflict on her own terms: locate the reactor core and its immense energy. She thought carefully about what she needed to do. She had to be exact, measured, patient. She had never returned energy to a nuclear reactor before. It wasn't just a printed circuit board or a power panel. It was precisely engineered and controlled nuclear fission. It was imperative that she avoid conditions that would lead to a nuclear accident. In starting her retaliatory strike, she assumed and relied on the technicians doing their work responsibly, monitoring the activity and manning the controls. A failure in watching the dials would potentially result in a catastrophe, killing many innocent people.

Focusing on the containment that emitted the power, she slowly began to raise the temperature inside it. With the gradual climb, technicians worked to manipulate the rods to adjust the temperature, but raising them did not lower the temperature. They looked upon the indicators with puzzlement, as the temperature continued to rise without reason. Calls were made to supervisors and engineers. It didn't make any sense. They continued to operate the dials on the containment, but nothing reduced the temperature that raised to a level activating alarms throughout the facility. This was now an emergency, quickly approaching a potentially lethal disaster.

The team executed an emergency shut down. To their amazement, the core temperature continued to rise. The scientist working on Katrina was startled by the alarms. He realized she was projecting the energy back to the plant. Frantic, he immediately shut down his equipment, taking away the energy from Katrina, and in turn, lowering the temperature to a safe reading. The scientist called Loom and informed him of the event. Dr. Loom turned on the equipment in his lab, connected with Katrina and communicated to her through the electrodes attached to his wired head band.

Katrina, we have shut down EM pulse. Please withdraw your focus on the reactor!

She received the signal from Loom and replied, *I am done being nice! You have no idea what I can do, and neither do I. Shall we find out together?*

Her spine began to burn. She rushed to fill the tub with water and ice. She jumped in, clothes and all.

No. We get it. We won't bother you or your family again, the scientist communicated.

You haven't seen me angry. You don't want to feel my anger. I could kill anyone of you anytime. Stay away. This is my final warning!

The scientist humbly accepted the conditions and shut down all his equipment. Katrina felt relief almost instantly and remained in the cold water for another ten minutes.

* * *

Emma once again had a look of surprise with a touch of terror. "Oh my God, Mom! You almost caused a nuclear meltdown?" She gave a short burst of laughter from the terror.

Katrina just looked at her. "I don't want to talk about it, Emma. I am not proud of it. Thinking about it sends a chill to this day. But

I am not leaving anything out with this talk tonight, even this part which I continue to be ashamed of."

"Go on. There can't be anything worse for you to tell me, right?"

Katrina didn't reply but continued with her stories.

* * *

After she got out of the tub, the phone rang. "Hello, Katrina. You did it! They won't touch you again!" an elated DD said.

"I am in so much pain now," Katrina said, her voice strained. "This pain is real, and it's as bad as before I had the enclosure and the biocircuit."

"Katrina, just like drugs, the electromagnetic pulses have an impact on your mind. And just like drugs, once the impact is gone, your brain will feel the stimulus gone, and you will go through withdrawal. The biocircuit will ensure you don't pass out or go into a coma. Keep it handy."

"What? Are you saying I'm addicted to the pulses now?"

"In sense, yes. The headaches and nausea will subside, but the spinal burn will never go away. You will not know when it will happen, and it doesn't show up on a schedule. I am not sure what activates it, but it will always be with you, so keep plenty of ice and a full tub of water on hand."

Katrina placed her head in her free hand and wept, tears falling into her ice bath.

"You will be fine," DD said in reassurance. "Use this time to recuperate."

"Have you done what you wanted to Dr. Loom?"

"As a matter of fact, I am going to do it tonight."

"What are you going to do?"

"I'll let you know after it's done. I don't like to share my tactics before I execute my plans."

DD told her he was proud of how she handled the last retaliation, showing control and discipline. He asked her how the biocircuit was working for her, and she indicated that she had felt a difference in her energy level after the retaliatory pulses. He promised he would call her the next day with the results of his visit with Dr. Loom. He wished her well as she felt another sharp pang in the side of her head.

* * *

...TURNING UP THE HEAT

It was about 3 a.m. Pacific Time. Loom had finally found sleep after replaying over and over again the incident at Rancho Seco. Back in Illinois, DD delighted in thought of what was about to transpire. His ability to project, to remote view, and to send energy was the stuff of comic book heroes. Devious in his approach, but not sinister, he focused his mind's energy on Loom in California. Distance was irrelevant. He used the realm of the spirits to enter his subject's mind during the dream state and produce a horrific nightmare. Then he communicated to him as if he was interrogating him.

"Loom. You have done your last experiment with my client. You are going to tell me everything you know about your operation. You are going to remain here with me until I am done questioning you. Do you understand?"

"Yes."

"Have you been involved in experiments with Katrina Hermann?"

"Yes."

"Are you still involved in experiments with Katrina Hermann?"

"No. I have decided to retreat in the face of the retaliation."

"Are others still involved with the experiment?"

"Yes. I believe others insist on attacking Katrina."

"Why was Katrina chosen for these experiments?"

"She was a client of Doctors Richards and Garson."

"Was there any other reason?"

"Her profile, based on interviews, indicated that she was psychologically ready to submit to authority."

"To what purpose? What interests your team about her?"

"We are developing bioelectromagnetic weapons. Multiple players are involved. At first, we harassed her to test the equipment. We were shocked at her resilience. No human should have survived what we put her through. She had the abilities we were trying to develop in our equipment—stronger. She's a threat! She's indestructible!"

"And she is my client. And I do not take your attacks on her lightly. What is your opinion of me?"

"Fear."

"Anything else?"

"Anger. I wish I could kill you."

"You want to kill me?"

"Yes."

"Why haven't you killed me yet?"

"We don't have your weaponry or ability."

"Who launched the EMP attack?"

"Brooks Johnson."

"Is he still involved in the experiment?"

"No. His specialty is EMP. He is a rogue member with the Department of Energy. We paid him."

"How many scientists are now involved with Katrina Hermann?"

"Four."

"Is Doctor Sweet directly involved with the experiment?"

"No, not anymore."

"Why did he withdraw?"

"The experiment was a failure. It was too costly and did not provide enough data."

"Did Katrina Hermann cause the fire in the lab?"

"Yes."

"Did your people know that she was the cause?"

"Yes."

"Are your people at the present time still monitoring her?"

"Yes."

"But you are no longer directly involved?"

"No, I removed myself from the activity."

"Have any of the people involved with your experiments died?"

"Yes."

"How many have died?"

"Three."

"Do you know who killed them?"

"Yes."

"Who did?"

"Katrina killed one of our younger scientists in training, and you killed the other two. You killed one of the best psychics we ever had. He was in the lab when your energy hit his heart. I hate you."

"The experiment is over, do you understand?"

"Yes."

"Your people will cease fire on Katrina Hermann, do you understand?"

"Yes."

"Or I will kill more, myself. I am not like Katrina. The death resulting from her retaliation was not intended. I, however, have been trained to kill. I have killed many, in various ways."

"I will try to stop them. Please don't kill anymore."

DD was satisfied with his interrogation. It ended with Loom in an abject state of fear, just the way it was designed. DD was confident the rogue CIA scientists would not bother Katrina anymore.

DD called Katrina the following morning to advise her that she would no longer be the subject of experiments by the rogue CIA scientists. Katrina asked for details regarding what he had done. Katrina was speechless as DD precisely and coldly described the nightmare interrogation. His voice resonated with pride and lusty enjoyment. When he was done, she humbly thanked him for ending the ordeal. DD omitted revealing to Katrina that he had killed two other scientists on the experiments. In his own sadistic manner, he thanked her for alerting him to the rogue cell.

"The *Company* is ambivalent when it comes to units that operate on their own, setting their own rules. Sometimes they follow a mission, but in doing so, they break a convention of order sometimes, drawing attention to themselves. If they get the job done without being traced back to the CIA, there is no effort to stop and capture them. The scientists who tortured you did the work on their own for their own personal gain.

"The CIA likes to know about people like you and me, but they won't touch us," he continued. "They know nothing good would come from it. They really are risk averse and prefer knowns rather than unknowns, especially when dealing with abilities beyond the norm. The CIA knew what was going on. They also knew that I knew. I'm not exactly rogue, but they don't control me either. The rogue scientists went beyond mission. The *Company* will get a complete report from me, tomorrow. Everyone who ever wanted to know about you, knows about you now. They also know that I am your ally. You are untouchable, Katrina. Enjoy your freedom."

The call ended with both assuring each other they would stay in touch. Katrina would eventually have to use her mind to defend herself again—but against other forces.

14
... THE DEPARTMENT OF ENERGY

Because of her connections, Katrina was hired as a specialist with a NASA lab in Nevada. Aside from the classified work she was involved in, her life was generally normal. She started her own blog, *Dragon Lady*. She posted information about the psychokinetic phenomenon and psychic activity in general, including remote viewing.

However, things were far less steady at home. Her mother's health was deteriorating from the advanced arthritis and Alzheimer's disease. Katrina had to care for her often and keep up with her young daughter, now approaching school age. Her father was little help with either burden. Since he lived by the motto "ignorance is bliss," he did not talk to Katrina about her condition. Katrina assured her parents that the episodes of harassment and torture were over.

"Are you sure, sweetheart?" asked her mother with a hopeful tone.

"I am quite confident they will not bother us again, Mom."

Though long retired, Commander Edwin Hermann remained under the watchful eyes of agents. He was never quite certain which agencies were involved, but he learned to be familiar with his daily activities being monitored by someone he would never know. He reasoned that perhaps Katrina was right: The torture was indeed over. However, he didn't think that they would stop watching her. "Just because they have stopped experimenting on you doesn't mean they have lost interest in you," he said, citing his own life experience. How long had it been since his work involving aliens? Three decades?

His words were unsettling and prophetic. Sure enough, just as everyone sat down for dinner, there was an untimely knock on the door. Katrina looked out the window and noticed a black sedan with federal plates and an older man in a suit standing on the stoop. She approached the door and opened it partially to talk to the stranger. He was a scientist from the Department of Energy, introducing himself simply as Leland. He asked if he could come inside to ask Katrina questions related to her job at NASA. Katrina let him in. Her parents remained seated, eating their dinner. Katrina led Leland to the living room.

He asked her questions about her ability and told her he had been made aware of her by a colleague who worked as a consultant with various government agencies, including NASA. Katrina did not hide the truth about her ability and responded to his technical questions. Convinced she was genuine, he mentioned the reason for his visit.

"Your ability and skills are much needed where I work," he said.

"You work at the DOE. What would they want from me and my psychokinetic skills?"

"We assist an agency that acquires technologies. The technologies are from exotic crafts that crashed," he stated bluntly.

Katrina's father overheard the statement, and it piqued his interest. He left the dinner table and entered the living room, where he joined them without asking for or receiving an invitation. It was his home and his daughter.

"I'm sorry, Commander Hermann. You'll have to leave. I am presenting extremely sensitive information," said Leland.

"I still have my TS clearance, and you are talking to my daughter about matters I worked on while active duty, so I have a need to know, too," continued Edwin as he walked toward the couch. He sat down next to Katrina to hear the rest of the conversation. Leland yielded to the retired intelligence officer.

Leland continued. "Over the course of decades of activity, the agency has amassed a collection of aerial vehicles not from this planet."

Edwin remained quiet, but listened to every word with interest.

"Through intense research, scientists have determined that some of those vehicles were operated organically, where the pilots interacted with the navigation and propulsion systems through thought patterns. We have found that normal humans are not able to access those systems with their thoughts in the way aliens do. Anecdotal evidence suggests the extraterrestrials use their minds to communicate. That kind of behavior points to their being psychic. We believe that the ETs that piloted the craft used their natural psychic abilities.

I am here because you have demonstrated that ability in your work at NASA."

"You want me to pilot a UFO?" Katrina asked.

"Not right away. The first step is to access the systems. We were thinking you may be able to at least access the controls before we actually have you pilot any craft. You would be guided by our scientists, who have been studying the craft for decades."

She tried to wipe the look of shock and disbelief off her face, maintain an even keel, but it was tough. The DOE officer's request was as much from outer space as the comments he was making. "There must be other psychics that can help you."

"There has been no one that could consistently do what you can. The folks that work alongside you at NASA are thoroughly impressed by the way it comes to you so effortlessly."

Katrina paused. Something inside began forewarning her of a huge risk in this endeavor. "I really don't know about this, Leland."

Leland arose from his chair. He explained he had printed material in his car that would explain more about what he told her. He left for brief moment and returned with a locked briefcase. Opening the case, he took out what appeared to be classified documents with titles related to UFO technology. He gave them to Katrina to read.

Edwin looked on with great interest. The discussion was conjuring memories of his work related to UFO technology under Naval Intelligence. Katrina was caught off balance from the sensitive information handed to her. On further inspection, the documents had been redacted and the place on the page where the security classification level would be noted was overwritten. The man also took out journals and technical papers concerning abnormal psychology.

"Take your time reading about this. Everything that I told you is described in detail in these pages. The UFO papers provide analysis on craft that is in our possession. There are technical descriptions and diagrams concerning the systems we are trying to access. The psychic journals have articles that you may find familiar to you, describing the ability in general terms. I will return in a couple weeks to take these documents back. I have been sent in the hope that you read them and that it would interest you in our mission to control those ships."

Katrina had little more to say. Her disbelief and shock passed, replaced by thoughtfulness, intrigue over the information the man left her, but she was certain that she wanted no part in any top-secret work that would eventually impinge on her freedoms. She knew this all too well from her father's experiences. The man thanked her for her time, bid his goodbyes to her family, and left.

The conversation might have surprised or shocked Katrina, but it intrigued Edwin tremendously. He was highly familiar with the material Leland provided.

"Katrina, I don't I need to convince you to not take his offer, regardless of what he presents to you."

"I know, Dad. I won't get mixed up with those people."

Edwin was curious and scanned over the documents Leland had left. He had seen much of the information before, under different covers and forms. Nothing seemed to have changed much since he left his job with Naval Intelligence. One document held his attention, though: a copy of a brief on MJ 12 from the Truman administration to the Eisenhower administration. It was dated 18 November 1952. At the bottom of the first page, he read:

The death of Secretary Forrestal on May 22, 1949, created a vacancy which remained unfulfilled until 01 August 1950, upon which General Walter B. Smith was designated as permanent replacement.

It brought back a bitter memory. Edwin returned the document in its original place of order. He stayed to talk to Katrina about the offer by the DOE.

"What do you know about this? Is this what you were involved in before you retired?" asked Katrina.

"I am not going to discuss anything beyond what Leland brought for you to read."

"Well, I prefer to give Emma and myself a more normal life than the one you put us through. There is nothing to read here. I'm not going to accept his offer."

"You should read the material he provided. You will not have the chance again. It may come in handy at NASA."

Katrina took her father's advice and began reading the documents. Edwin was surprised to hear that Katrina still harbored resentment about growing up in the family of a high-level intelligence officer.

As promised, the man from the DOE arrived a couple weeks later to get Katrina's response and to retrieve his documents.

"I'm sorry, Leland," she said, disappointing him with her decision while her father stood by as support. "I just want to lead as normal a life as I can without wondering if someone wants to eliminate me because they are suspicious of my behavior."

"I could not let my daughter involve herself in highly classified work," Edwin added. "I know what it is like to be followed everywhere you go. She shouldn't have to wonder if someone is listening to her conversation or going through her trash. That is the kind of life I had, and because of that life, my family suffered." Katrina and her father looked at each other. Katrina's mother overheard her husband from where she sat in the dining room.

Leland replied coldly. "Edwin Hermann, Commander, US Navy, retired. A rarity, being an officer without a college diploma—a true *mustang*. Your record is still highly classified. It is as if you did not exist." He glanced at Katrina.

"I think we have made it clear, Mr. Leland. She has no desire to get into that line of work. She has a good position at NASA," Edwin said, completely unswayed by Leland's soft attempt at intimidation.

But the DOE officer wasn't finished. "We would offer her a generous salary comparable to a high, civil-servant pay grade. She would be making more than twice what she is making at NASA right now."

"Your offer is generous, Leland, but it still is not worth the loss of my freedom and the threat to my life, should I leave. My decision is final," Katrina reiterated.

Disappointed, the man took his journals and papers, placed them back in the briefcase, locked it, and stood to leave.

But not without a parting remark. "Katrina, you should be well aware by now that we know so much about you already. We know more about you than you know about yourself. You're famous. It doesn't matter what decision you make, dear. You will never lead a 'normal' life. Someone will always be watching you."

Leland's words chilled Katrina to the bone, not because of their threatening nature. Because she knew they were true.

15
... PROFESSIONAL DEVELOPMENT

During her off hours, Katrina continued to write in her blog. To Katrina's delight, it attracted sensible and knowledgeable people that indulged in engrossing conversation, exchanging ideas. New contacts through the blog allowed Katrina to enter another world related to psychic ability. This included Steven Aftergood, head of the Project on Government Secrecy at the Federation of American Scientists, who approached her through a private message.

Aftergood worked to reduce the scope of national security secrecy and to promote public access to government information. He informed her of a program that was declassified in 1995 called Stargate, the code name for a small, secret US Army unit at Fort Meade, Maryland, established in 1978 by the Defense Intelligence Agency. According to Mr. Aftergood, the mission was to investigate psychic phenomena and its applications in military and intelligence gathering. He mentioned to Katrina that the project primarily dealt with remote viewing. He also told her that the project was terminated after a CIA report concluded it had not been useful in any intelligence operation. Now, Aftergood was interested in what Katrina would write in her blog about remote viewing and psychokinetics.

Katrina kept a lot of the details to herself. She maintained the blog to see if she could find other people who harbored or utilized special abilities. She had no interest in making contacts with people in positions of authority. Aftergood's information provided Katrina the first evidence of remote viewing as part of a US Government program. Yielding to an abundance of caution, she never went further in communicating with Mr. Aftergood. The blog attracted shadowy people, too. An Army psychologist often visited the blog and left cryptic messages for contact. Katrina had a bad feeling about him.

That wasn't all. As she continued working at NASA, Katrina noticed she was being followed by the same vehicle up to the security gate. She notified the guard at the entrance that she was being stalked. Shortly afterward, the incident was reported to the security officer. From that point on, she was no longer tailed. Coincidentally, the Army psychologist left the blog at the same time.

The most impactful contact she made on the blog was with Dr. Lauren Beauchard, a professor at the University of Nevada, who told her more about remote viewing and suggested to Katrina that she attend formal courses on the subject. Katrina was drawn to the prospect of communicating with a well-respected authority on the topic. For two weeks, she attended a course in Boulder City, taught by the doctor. Upon stellar performance and completion of the course, Dr. Beauchard offered Katrina a position at the Sierra Remote Viewers (SRV). She was still able to keep her job with NASA. Through her father's benefits, Katrina was able to place Emma at the childcare center at Beale.

There was a lot of work at SRV. One of the active clients was Robert Bigelow, founder of Bigelow Aerospace, and ranking member at MUFON (The Mutual UFO Network). Katrina's first assignment was to predict the socioeconomic and political environment of Eastern Europe for the next two years. She put together a 200-page report that included articles and papers researched through the internet and with the aid of her psychic ability.

SRV also received work to find missing persons and runaways. One woman approached SRV and requested assistance in finding her son. The mother met Katrina and Lauren for a dinner.

"Dr. Beauchard, my son is a naturalist. He is a student at Brigham Young. Last weekend, he went on an extended hike by himself camping in the Uinta Wasatch Cache National Forest. His roommate told us he didn't return like he was supposed to for classes Monday," explained the mother.

"We can't guarantee anything. If he is alive, Katrina would be able to locate him," added Dr. Beauchard.

"He was caught in bad weather, but he is an experienced hiker," acknowledged the mother.

While the mother was explaining more to Dr. Beauchard, Katrina searched but could not recognize a life signature. When the mother left the table, Katrina conveyed what she sensed to Dr. Beauchard.

"Lauren, I can't give the mother a definitive answer. I need more time. I'm not comfortable talking about it here and now."

"Is having the mother here a distraction? Are you having trouble focusing?"

Katrina nodded solemnly. When the mother returned, Lauren was able to convince her that there were too many distractions for Katrina and that it would be best to let Katrina work under her own preferred conditions. After the mother left, Lauren returned her attention to Katrina.

"Our clients expect prompt service. My company has an excellent reputation, with reviews by famous and powerful people and organizations I cannot reveal. This mother came to us because she knows someone, someone influential."

"I'm sorry Dr. Beauchard. I couldn't find her son's signature. It wasn't even faint. I am afraid her son is not alive. I didn't want to tell her here in this public place. It would have been terrible for her and for others to witness her reaction."

Lauren agreed. The next day, Lauren reluctantly called the mother to inform her that Katrina had not been able recognize a life signature for her son.

Through SRV, Katrina attended a UFO conference in Laughlin, Nevada, where she was introduced to such notables as Colonel John Alexander, author and leading expert on nonlethal weaponry; Lyn Buchanan, part of the defunct Project Stargate; author and researcher Richard Dolan; Dean Radin, leading researcher and founder of the Institute of Noetics; and investigative reporter, Linda Moulton Howe. She was in awe of all the celebrity authors and researchers assembled in one conference. When she introduced herself and explained why she was there, hardly anyone showed interest. Many of the personalities and celebrities had written books or had been on radio shows. Katrina was new to the scene, an unknown claiming to possess amazing attributes. Katrina felt like she was in high school again, trying to socialize with the popular crowd. She was delighted to meet such a cast of people but wished someone had shown interest in what she offered.

Another major client to SRV was the Department of Defense. A rushed request came to search for a downed Pakistani pilot, last having radio contact over the Himalaya Mountains. The order came in just as it was time to close the office. The DoD gave SRV four hours to find the pilot. Katrina reviewed the assignment sheet and looked back at Lauren, eyes and mouth wide open. Lauren told her the time constraint was based on the chance for survival. Katrina got very little information to help her. She received information on the type of aircraft, the pilot's name and rank, and the last place he made contact over the region. Katrina and a team of three worked the case. At the beginning of the session, team members were unable to find the pilot's life signature and ascertained it was likely he had not survived. However, through remote viewing, Katrina picked up a sighting of the pilot huddling in an ice cave he had built for himself. She notified the DoD contact that she found him—alive. While awaiting a response, she continued to zero in on his location.

Soon, the response came—a fax of the photograph of the pilot. It matched the image she saw in her viewing work. She was able to pinpoint the location in the mountains and faxed a map with his location to the DoD. The next couple hours were extremely stressful for her. Because she had found him alive, as well as because of her maternal instincts, she assumed responsibility for his safety. She also realized she was helpless in this situation, not having knowledge of the location of the pararescue unit and not being able to communicate with the downed pilot. Since she could sense his energy signature, she decided she would try to ping him softly as a form of communication. It required a precise level of energy. Too strong of a ping would level a jolt, and it could potentially kill him. She was conflicted and frustrated to possess the ability but not the knowledge of how to use it safely. She decided it was too risky and continued to check on his signature.

Four hours later, a fax arrived at the office. It was a photograph of the search team—and the rescued pilot. Katrina was relieved and inwardly joyous in being able to help save a life, instead of taking one.

Katrina's success as a remote viewer attracted the attention of many, including a group of desperate people representing organizations and countries not aligned with the interests of the United States.

16

... AL-QAEDA

Katrina continued working for SRV, performing admirably in various domestic and international assignments. She enjoyed the work and success rate so much that she opted to leave her job at NASA to work full-time at SRV. Her steady, respectable income allowed her to contribute toward home nursing care for her mother, who continued to deteriorate in health. In addition, she was able to raise her daughter, who was now enrolled in Lone Tree Elementary School at Beale. For the first time in ages, she felt like a normal mother doing what normal single parents do—wrapping their lives around their kids and their jobs.

She continued writing her blog, gaining more followers and subscribers, including some considered to be on the fringe of society. She found herself often tempering their input of extraordinary conspiracy theories. Some cultish members would post strange, somewhat oblique messages daily. Out of a crop of those messages, she picked out an intriguing one from a cousin.

Kent Williams worked in a cryptology office for NSA, in Missouri. He relayed to her that a prominent engineer from Pakistan, Iqbal Ali, was interested in contacting her. Ali had been following Katrina's blog and had been asking Kent questions. Katrina trusted Kent and passed on her contact information. The Pakistani engineer called her shortly afterward, a proud and boastful man, but the stories he told revealed that he was astonishingly resourceful and influential. For example, somehow, Ali knew details about her cousin's private life. During the phone call, he imparted his concern regarding her cousin, Kent.

"Ms. Katrina, it is a pity about your cousin. He is such a brilliant engineer. However, it seems he is a transvestite. This would certainly harm his professional career if the information was to be exposed publicly. Don't you agree?"

Iqbal's accusation took Katrina by surprise. *Who was this man? How did he get that information? Was it true anyway? If he knows this secret about Kent, what does he know about me?* The more she thought about it, the more it felt wrong. Katrina had heard rumors about Kent. He never talked to her about his private life.

"Before I engage in any discussion concerning my abilities," she said, "you will have to tell me more about yourself. Who you are ... your family ... what brought you into the work you do ... why is it important to you ... what your objectives are."

The next day, Ali delivered his résumé. Among his many interesting positions, he served as adviser to the Ministry of Defense in Libya. He also assisted in the development of young Muammar Gaddafi, Brotherly Leader of Libya. While working with Libya, Ali was trained as a terrorist by the East German Secret Police, the Stasi. There, he came in contact with East Germans that would engage in operations against the CIA and Mossad. In East Germany, he learned to hate Jewish people.

This is crazy! What am I doing interacting with this person? He's dangerous! Thanks a lot, Kent. Now what? Who knows what he could do? Who he knows? What would he do if I denied him? He hates? He hates Jewish people? God—that so irrational. Maybe it's best I keep tabs on him I'll just have to be very cautious.

* * *

"Jesus Christ, Mom! This is unbelievable! It's like you lived in a spy novel."

"People with my ability are targets. They see us as walking weapons to be controlled or replicated. Organizations that look for that have a dark side, making arrangements with intelligent but troubled characters who will trample on other people's rights to get what they want."

"I don't think there is one person you have described that would convince me to be friends with them. As soon as Ali told you about working with East German Stasi, I would have thought you would have left."

"Keep your friends close and your enemies closer."

Katrina resumed.

***

In spite of the red flags, Katrina continued to correspond with Ali. Over time, Ali disclosed that he worked at a laboratory in Islamabad, researching the psychokinetic phenomenon and working on electromagnetic weapon systems. He explained that the lab was built with the assistance of the United States. He bragged his lab possessed billions of dollars of equipment bought with funds supposed to be dedicated for Pakistani military aid to counter terrorism. Ali expressed deep interest in Katrina's torture experiences, especially, how she was able to repel the energy pulses. From his inquiries, it became apparent to Katrina that Ali's lab possessed similarities with the labs operated by Doctors Sweet and Loom. Ali asked deeper, detailed questions about the episodes and what she had felt. When he sensed her reluctance to divulge information, he would change the subject or end the call. During subsequent calls, he continued to press for the information, but Katrina was mindful not to give him details on her ability, the impact on her, or how she was able to retaliate. Katrina remained firm in her resolve to protect the knowledge that could be used against her in an electromagnetic attack.

Ali also boasted of being friends with Osama bin Laden and maintaining contacts within the Taliban and Al-Qaeda. *Oh, no,* she thought. *Ali is a serious, serious threat. If I'm being monitored, my contact with him is certainly going to raise suspicion.* She also surmised her cousin was a security risk. She wondered how much Kent knew about Ali.

Ali restated his ties to the CIA. He confided he was an arms supplier, banned from entering the United States. Again, she heard alarms in her head. *This guy couldn't be any more dangerous!*

Katrina called her father for advice on Ali and how to deal with him. She rarely discussed her work with Edwin, but Ali's disclosures and ties raised enough red flags to surround the UN Headquarters in New York. She needed his feedback, his expertise. Katrina described Ali and his background as Edwin listened intently.

"What do you think, Dad?"

"How did this guy find you?"

"My blog. I have met some great people through that blog, but there are a lot of questionable types too."

"So, you brought this upon yourself," Edwin said.

Katrina brushed off the typical remark of a stern, emotionally detached father. "Not exactly. Ali found me on the blog, then he somehow knew Kent."

"Williams? Your cousin at the NSA?"

"Yeah. Kent told me that Ali wanted to contact me. I told Kent he could give my number to Ali."

"Conversing with that man gives anyone monitoring you reason to suspect you are a threat. Drop him," Edwin said, his voice full of warning and caution.

"But how?"

"You mentioned he hates Jews. There's your out. Mention you have a Jewish background. I know these guys. They will cut off a limb if they find themselves chained to a Jew."

There wasn't much else to discuss. Katrina thanked her father for the advice. In a not-so-subtle way, he told her to discontinue the blog. Katrina did not acknowledge the admonition.

Katrina followed through with her father's instructions. In a subsequent call with Ali, she revealed to him she had Jewish ancestors. The information incensed Ali, causing him to turn on her and declare he would make it a mission to attack her. He stopped all communication with her. In turn, as a prudent measure, Katrina blocked him on her blog.

Katrina was relieved to lose contact with the underworld figure. She returned to her simpler life and her not-so-regular job. Everything was going just fine until she was attacked again. It was similar to the rogue CIA assaults from several years before. Now, though, these invasions of her solitude angered her more than they physically hurt her. In anticipation, she hurriedly filled her tub as pulses and waves began bombarding her brain. The sensation differed from the cranial tempest from previous battles. This time, pulses, hums, and drones alternated. A half-decade of progress made technology so advanced, there was no need for amplifiers or generators in her vicinity. She found it difficult to collect and process the information necessary to lead her to the source of attack.

Through the confusing oscillation of the energy waves, she was still able to read thought patterns in her tormentors regarding her rescue of a downed Pakistani pilot in the Himalayas, years ago. She was surprised to discover the incident was being used as a motive for her attack. Her attackers were Pakistani. They communicated in Pashtun, but she was able to read the patterns because thought is not affected by language barriers. They accused her of aiding the enemy. Katrina reasoned she was dealing with a terrorist group in Pakistan, possibly aligned with Al-Qaeda. She heard laughter as they applied the electromagnetic pulses to her brain. She was able to read one of the minds, boasting she was good target practice. Staying focused, she recognized satellites in the network and the energy waves coming from somewhere in Nevada, near the Utah border. The activity was sporadic and didn't allow her enough time to pinpoint the location.

The next several days brought more sporadic electromagnetic attacks from other sources. Pulses continued to shift randomly. Energy waves increased and decreased without pattern. At times, electromagnetic oceans of waves pummeled her, followed by calm hums. Pain echoed from every side of her skull. These operatives were clever.

Just when she was about to return fire, the energy was shut down. The pain spread to her nervous system, where she unexpectedly experienced a disconnection, disrupting motions. The attacks sometimes felt like tiny splinters penetrating deep around her head and her spine like she was ravaged by shingles. Rage built inside her. They continued to hit her hard, then just before she could retaliate, they would cease all activity. They weren't predictable like Doctor Sweet and his team. They knew when she worked and timed their attacks to coincide with her work schedule.

Often, she felt ionization in the air. It would be accompanied by a signal in her mind indicating interference or surveillance. The application of the signal was unique. The newness, the lack of familiarity, shook her to the extent of losing concentration or behaving absent-mindedly. It impacted her performance at work. Something about the system did not allow her to use electromagnetic waves to retaliate. All Katrina could do was observe. She was impotent. Her *gun* had no bullets. And when she was ready to fire, she couldn't pull the trigger. For the first time in a long time, she felt powerless. There was no refuge. They attacked her at will anytime, anywhere. She was completely at their mercy, unable to plan for interruptions to her day-to-day activities.

Katrina decided she needed help and called her old mentor, DD.

"Katrina! How are you? You're not under attack, are you? Loom and Sweet would be foolish to hit you again."

"DD—it's not Loom or Sweet. I have a new nemesis: Al-Qaeda."

"Oh. Are you sure it's Al-Qaeda? You're being electromagnetically attacked by them?"

"Yes—Pakistanis. They are being led by an engineer, Iqbal Ali. He's dangerous. He's a self-described terrorist, Stasi-trained."

"How did you find this gem? Why is he attacking you?"

Katrina explained how he contacted her through her NSA cousin.

"DD—these guys are smart. They don't pulse the energy long enough for me to trace the sources. They know exactly how much time I need to absorb the energy and release it. They shut it down before the energy level reaches the yield point. Can you help?"

"Katrina—I could only help locate the source if I am being targeted. Give me some time to research Ali. Maybe the *Company* has information that could be used to identify the sources. How are you holding up? I sense everything is well balanced in you—no damage."

"I'm fine. The harassment is unpredictable and affecting my work at SRV. Thanks for your help, DD."

The following day, DD imparted what he had learned about Iqbal Ali through his intelligence sources. Ali was indeed a CIA asset. DD was warned not to divulge too much about Ali. He still had a critical assignment in Pakistan assisting the CIA. DD warned Katrina that an attack on Ali would be an attack on the CIA. He advised Katrina to focus on Ali's facility rather than the man himself. "Katrina, the torture team is in Islamabad, but the power source is in Abbottabad. The culprits are Pakistanis aligned with Al-Qaeda, but I detected two US advisers—possibly rogue CIA," he added.

"Do you see Ali in that group?"

There was brief silence.

"DD?"

"No. He is not in the group at Islamabad." In order to divert her attention, DD said, "Read me, Katrina. You should be able to visualize the energy source in Abbottabad."

DD projected his thoughts and visions to Katrina, allowing her to envision the facility. It was a simple concrete block, windowless building in the older part of the city. She described it to DD accurately. "It's easy pickings, Katrina. Pour yourself a glass of red wine and enjoy it while you destroy them."

This time, there was no emotion, no signature cackle. His choice of words made Katrina chuckle nervously. Katrina thanked him for his help. DD indicated that he would monitor her to make sure she was alright.

Before they ended the call, DD shared more information about the lab in Islamabad. He described a room with a dozen video monitors being watched by bearded men. One man was watching pornography. Another appeared to be watching a feed with a view of the inside of a cave. The figure in the feed was tall, wearing traditional Arab garb. DD told her it was Osama bin Laden. Another screen had a view of a Pakistani Army outpost.

Later that night, Katrina was the victim of two brief attacks. The Hermann Circuit was able to reduce the impact to her body. The following morning, Katrina took her circuit to work and confided in Lauren, letting her in on what was happening to her.

"A blog can be of great benefit, and at the same time, it can subject you to threats from the outside, you never knew existed. SRV will not get involved in anyone's personal conflicts. We are not legally set up for that. I cannot allow us to be exposed like that," Lauren said.

"I understand. I'll try not to let it interfere with my job."

Katrina waited to exact her retaliation. With the location of the energy source in Abbottabad, she hugged her biocircuit and focused on the transformer emitting the highest amount of power. She projected the energy back to the transformer, causing it to overheat, then erupt in flames and explode. The explosion caused a siren to activate, and people in the adjacent buildings ran out into the street. People feared it was a terrorist attack. It drew attention to the austere industrial building surrounded by late model German sedans. The occupants exited the facility quickly and left in their cars. That incident marked the end of the harassment by the Al-Qaeda operatives.

Her run-in with Ali, and his influence on rogue CIA cells sympathetic to Al-Qaeda, did not end with her retaliatory attack on Abbottabad. The CIA preserved relations with members of the Taliban and Al-Qaeda, formerly part of the Mujahadeen, who fought as freedom fighters against the Soviets in Afghanistan in the late 1970s and 1980s. The Mujahadeen transformed from freedom fighters against the Soviets to insurgents in order to promote Islamic extremism in Southwest Asia. Afghans and Pakistanis recruited by the CIA to aid the Mujahadeen remained loyal to their friends that turned to Al-Qaeda and the Taliban. Many of those ex-CIA members went rogue and remained in the country as sleeper cells. Ali knew a good number of those people and used his connections to continue to torment Katrina.

This time, he was able to activate sleepers and provide them the equipment to carry out his revenge. The equipment wasn't as sophisticated as the equipment or tactics used in Pakistan. It seemed to be a hastily organized attempt to punish her. The attacks, issued simultaneously from various sources, infuriated her. Once again, she wasn't able to recognize any one location to focus on. The attacks were a staccato beat on her mind with varied frequencies and pulses. It was not enough to cause damage but enough to be disturbing.

Katrina called DD for help again. This time, there was no answer. She was blind without him, on her own now. The attacks occurred at all hours of the day at work. It was getting difficult to function with the distractions. Their tactics were working. The attacks affected how she related with people, exhibiting a short temper and a lack of patience. It was affecting her performance at SRV. She was dependent on the biocircuit wherever she went. Katrina would get intermittent images and messages indicating that the operators were not trained in the equipment and that there were other agents assisting. After a couple weeks of what she recognized as target practice, Katrina caught a break from a less careful operator. Recognizing a clear, strong signal, she focused the energy back to the source. She recognized it as a rare chance, and she did not measure her response. From her station at SRV, she returned fire.

Her target was an abandoned mine near Ely, Nevada, close to Salt Lake City. A lone metal-roofed shed was its only structure. She followed the energy to its source, deep underground. With the next burst, she sent the energy back to the underground lab where she sensed an older man in a plaid shirt watching the dials with someone that could have been a trainee. The energy blast on the equipment surprised both men. Sparks flew from the panels on the cabinet, and the monitor popped. The event sent the older man into cardiac arrest, killing him. Not knowing who was responsible for the operation of the abandoned mine lab made Katrina uneasy.

* * *

"You killed a second person?"

"It was an accident. I intended to damage only the equipment."

"So it's true. You really had no control over what you were doing? What about now, Mom? Do you still have the ability? Have you done anything recently?"

If I use my mind to manipulate energy, it may cause me to go into a coma. No, dear. I can't take that risk. Besides, having Robert as someone who can protect me means I don't have to be on the defensive anymore."

* * *

Next to her, one of her coworkers sensed the event and glared at Katrina. Katrina knew she had not killed the man intentionally but would not be able to provide proof. Word reached Lauren, and Katrina was called into the office.

"Katrina, you are an effective and accurate remote viewer—the best we have, but I have to let you go," Lauren said.

Katrina was stunned. "I had no intentions of killing that man. He died of a heart attack from the return of the electromagnetic energies."

Lauren shook her head, as sad about her decision as she was resolute about the reasons for making it. "I talked to you about this earlier. We had an agreement. Now, you have exposed us to a potential wrongful death suit. This is not a decision on your performance, it is a business decision based on risks. You are too risky. That probably won't be the last time you are attacked; we cannot let it happen again while you are employed here. Our operation is under surveillance and harassment by your enemies and their allies. We are not equipped to fight that battle, and that is not our business model. I am terminating you effective today. I am sorry. There are no other options. I wish you success in your future work."

Katrina removed her personal effects from her workstation and left, never to return to the remote viewing role. She returned to her supervisor at NASA, who gladly rehired her.

17

... THE OIL SHEIK

Ten years later...

Katrina relished in the pleasure of working in a NASA special projects office for the past decade after being let go by Sierra Remote Viewing. She was now in a supervisory position, assisting in recruiting people that demonstrated psychic abilities. The promotion allowed her to leave her parents' home in Grass Valley and move into a trailer on the outskirts of Fernley, Nevada. Her daughter, Emma, was a teen. Despite Emma's encroaching adulthood, Katrina kept her insulated from mom's work and extracurricular activities. Whenever Emma noticed her mother take an occasional ice bath, Katrina explained it invigorated her and tightened her skin.

In spite of her father's advice, and how the blog led to her dismissal from SRV, Katrina continued to write, which continued to grow in popularity. As an added benefit, it helped her find recruits for NASA. However, it also was a method by which people with ulterior motives could contact her.

Talal-al-Elahi was a loyal subscriber to her blog. He was an Iraqi oil sheik living in Switzerland. Like Katrina, Elahi was an electrical engineer. Some people were intrigued by Katrina and what she wrote about her psychic ability. Others were obsessed. That was Elahi. Katrina had learned about Elahi before he ever made contact with her, through his second wife, Zia. Katrina befriended her through a meditation group on social media. Zia came from an aristocratic Filipino family. Katrina felt the need to call Zia about Elahi.

"Zia—your husband has been contacting me, and he is making me uncomfortable. He asks me personal questions and he flirts."

"I'm so sorry, Katrina. That is the way he is since I married him."

"Why don't you leave him?"

"I'm afraid. He has a network of people that are like servants to him. He will know where I go and will take revenge on me."

"He boasts a lot about himself, his business, and his wealth."

"Katrina—he's a narcissist. He has a grand image of himself believing he descended from the Anunnaki."

"Anunnaki?" asked Katrina.

"There is a belief held by many that they created the human race as a slave race to mine gold and diamonds. Anyway, be careful in your relationship. His first wife successfully ran away. It injured his pride, and he still curses her memory."

Katrina thanked Zia for the talk and her honesty. Zia offered to be available any time Katrina wanted to talk.

With each new correspondence, Katrina was more drawn to his exotic background. She replied to his inquiries regularly and promptly. Her responses encouraged him to try to seduce her with examples of his outlandish lifestyle. Elahi started by sending her photos of his residences: a villa in Geneva, an apartment in Dubai, a beach house in Bermuda. He followed with his collection of cars—his favorite a restored red 1965 Corvette Stingray. He completed his show and tell by sending photos of his yacht and his helicopter. Elahi told Katrina that he admired her for her courage and that she seemed to be a highly intelligent woman. Katrina wrote a passage in her Dragon Lady blog without identifying Elahi:

> *I met a very interesting wealthy man through this blog. He's been sending me photos of his residences in Europe, Asia, and the Caribbean. He also has a yacht and a helicopter. He told me is an oil sheik. Wow. I'm not sure why he approached me. I hope it's not because he wants to have a relationship. I have no desire to get into something like that now. I will keep you informed of any updates. DL*

Elahi was less interested in romance and more interested in Katrina's abilities. He conveyed to her that he dabbled in psychokinetics with technology, not through an ability. He also revealed that he had a place in Geneva, Switzerland, because his son was an engineer at CERN. Elahi informed Katrina that his son also had a deep interest in her work and her ability, doing research on bioelectromagnetic technology. He told her that his son would offer her a position at CERN. That specific research was being funded by Prince Turki Al-

Faisal Al Saud. It turned out that Elahi was also part of the OPEC oil cartel working with the Saudis.

Elahi offered to pay for her tickets so she and Emma could join him in Switzerland. He began to pursue her romantically. Katrina was used to exchanging technical information. She even tolerated his brash exhibitionist behavior. When he shifted to sending intimate messages, she felt no enjoyment. She wasn't even curious. She relayed to Zia updates on Elahi and his messages. Zia continued to caution Katrina about Elahi and his abusive character. Elahi's obsession with Katrina and her ability caused him to zero in on his objective. He persisted. Recognizing Katrina was not moved by words of love, he eventually refrained from wooing her with serenades. Elahi shifted to a more pragmatic approach, selling Katrina on a life of bounty, better security from threats, and wealth to extend to her family. His reasonable style seemed to yield positive responses.

Katrina recognized Elahi offered a tempting option to exposure to unknown and known external threats. There was so much imbalance surrounding her. At times she preferred to have a more predictable, stable life for her and Emma. In spite of Zia's advice, Katrina thought Elahi would treat her differently.

. She wanted so badly to be able to trust someone that she let her guard down. He convinced her to convert to Islam, taking the Shahada, a ceremony to declare that she would pursue Islam as her faith. She went to a mosque near Reno to learn more. The prospects of living a sumptuous lifestyle for once, and leaving behind the constant threats from unknown assailants, appealed to her greatly. She would no longer have to fear for the safety of her daughter. Would living in Switzerland make her free from the rogue CIA and Al-Qaeda.? It was a hopeful thought. Staying in Nevada had a higher risk.

Katrina pursued starting yet another chapter. She was leaving for adventure, for companionship. For safety. She was going somewhere other than the desert of Nevada and eastern California. Elahi would pay for the trailer she had moved into recently, as well as the massive costs of her mother's care.

Not surprisingly, Edwin Hermann was skeptical. He contacted his nephew, Kent Williams, at NSA and asked for a check on Mr. Elahi.

While Katrina was finalizing her plans for her life-changing trip, Kent initiated a routine security check on Elahi. He found unsettling information. There were numerous incidents involving domestic disturbances and an ongoing investigation involving human trafficking. Elahi was considered suspicious but not dangerous in the profile. Kent contacted Katrina and convinced her to meet him in Switzerland before meeting Elahi.

Elahi learned of Kent's plan through a mole, likely the same mole that had informed Iqbal Ali of Kent's private life. The news upset Elahi. He would not relinquish control of the situation, especially if it impacted his objective of taking control of Katrina and her powers.

Forces beyond conventional explanation resulted in a complete reversal for Katrina. As her plane was ready to take off, a most bizarre event took place. The plane was still at the terminal, awaiting takeoff, when an anomalous fog descended upon the airfield. It was so encumbering that it impacted the tower's visibility. This caused air traffic control to delay her flight indefinitely.

Katrina decided to place a call to Elahi to advise him of the delay. She dialed one number. It was not in service. She dialed a second number. Again, not in service. She tried the other two numbers she held. Neither were in service. A feeling of uneasiness crept over her. She called her friend, a deputy sheriff at Lyon County, for help. With the flight still delayed, the deputy made the necessary calls to allow Katrina and Emma to deplane and retrieve their bags. Thus ended her dreams of a life of abundance and her relationship with Elahi.

So she thought.

* * *

"OK, Mom. That story really creeped me out. It's so not like you. A rich narcissistic polygamist? You were going to convert to Islam?"

"I know. I know. But now I look back, and I have to laugh. I think I just wanted to leave Nevada with the assurance that Grandma and Grandpa would be taken care of, and that you would have a life of wonder in Europe."

"But what about you, Mom? What about *your* happiness?"

"I don't know. I suppose I figured that I went through so much and survived, that I would be able to handle anything. It also could simply be that it had been a long time since a man took interest in me like Elahi did."

"I need another glass of wine," Emma went back to kitchen to pour herself some emotional support. "Please tell me it's not going to get weirder."

"I didn't get involved with anyone like that anymore. Things got so much better after meeting Mary Ellen and then Robert."

18

... THE AWAKENED ORPHAN

Katrina spent as much time with her mother as she could. Together, intrigued after playing the Jewish ruse to shake Ali, they decided to trace her lineage. They discovered Cherokee blood in her ancestry. Katrina, anxious to learn more, visited web sites concerning issues particular to Native Americans. At one site, she entered into in-depth online chats with a Jicarilla Apache woman living on a reservation in Dulce, New Mexico. Hiding her identity in the public eye, the Jicarilla Apache woman called herself The Awakened Orphan. Katrina enjoyed the chats with the woman and invited her to visit her own blog. They engaged in discussing spirituality and psychic phenomena.

At first, they communicated on a weekly basis. Katrina would tell the woman about real life events related to remote viewing, and the woman would tell Katrina about her own experiences involving the use of her mind to gather information and heal spirits. Katrina would discuss the science behind her remote viewing skills and the woman would point out the spiritual aspect of the mind. The discussion allowed them to learn from each other. It wasn't long before they were talking on daily basis.

Each day, Katrina looked forward to her chats with the Apache woman from Dulce. Likewise, the woman was enthralled by her conversations with Katrina. As time passed, the relationship and trust grew. The woman from Dulce privately revealed her name to Katrina: Mary Ellen Velarde.

In one chat session, their spiritual bond strengthened. Mary Ellen asked about Katrina's abilities, and Katrina offered a demonstration.

"Mary Ellen, you haven't described your home. You live in a trailer just off the main street in town. You are sitting in your bedroom at the end of the trailer. I love all the dream catchers and crystals! Is that a deerskin around the mirror? Nice touch!"

"You are amazing! You really can remote view!—so effortlessly! Ok—my turn. I don't have that accuracy you have, and I really have to sit still and have something about you in my hand to get even close to what you can do. But...I can work with spirits and people's energy centers."

"The chakras?"

"Right. Now I read people only if they let me. So, will you allow me to read your spirit and chakras?"

"Please. I haven't had that done in a long time, and I'm sure you will do a thorough job."

"Remember what I told you about the energy centers a while ago. You have seven. I will focus on the ones that are most out of balance."

Katrina obliged, still not sure of what to expect. She listened intently as Mary Ellen described details in the healing process, after which she indicated she was ready to begin.

Mary Ellen sat composed and silent as she began to read Katrina. Katrina respected the silence and remained still, assuming movement would disturb Mary Ellen. It did not take long for Mary Ellen to offer her first observations.

"Wow, Katrina, the guides tell me you have been through a lot. The electromagnetic pulses you have endured the past decade have corrupted your energy centers. All except your third eye chakra and your 'throat' chakra need to be healed. This is my specialty. You will notice a big difference after I work on you. Your 'root' chakra seems to be the second dominant energy, so it won't take much to balance that."

Mary Ellen instructed Katrina to close her eyes and imagine her "root" chakra as a rotating red energy center, like a pinwheel. She had her visualize good things in nature that are red such as strawberries, roses, poppies, and tomatoes. Katrina followed her instructions. Mary Ellen noticed the energy center attain balance while she continued to apply her spiritual energy to heal Katrina.

The next chakra that needed repair was her "will" chakra, the weakest of her energy centers, as she was constantly bombarded and abused. Ten years or more of electromagnetic abuse eroded her willpower, restricting her ability to grow independently and confidently. Hence, hugging tight to her parents.

Mary Ellen applied a similar technique to help Katrina. She had her concentrate on the color orange as it existed in nature: pumpkins, persimmon, tulips, zinnias, and of course, oranges. Katrina's visualization was once again, effective. Mary Ellen began to sense a higher positive energy from that center. She continued to monitor until she was satisfied with the balance. Encouraged by the progress, Mary Ellen worked on the next energy center, the "solar plexus" chakra. This energy had been low since her budding relationship with Elahi fell apart. Mary Ellen instructed her to visualize all the good things in nature that are yellow: lemons, squash, fields of dandelions. As with the other chakras, the energy center began to heal and emit a sustainable level of high energy.

"How are you feeling?" asked Mary Ellen.

"I feel a subtle change. Perhaps it is because I want to feel that way."

"Well, the healing cannot happen without your intentions. That is why I was asking you to visualize the colors in nature. Do you want to take a break or continue?"

"Let's continue," Katrina said, already encouraged by the results and her innate trust of the Jicarilla Apache woman.

Mary Ellen proceeded to the higher chakras, beginning with the "heart." *Anahata.* As Mary Ellen discovered, Katrina devolved into cynicism and mistrust with every negative person she met. Even her remote viewing teacher, Lauren, who she thought understood her more than her parents understood her, turned out to hurt Katrina by letting her go at SRV. Mary Ellen sensed the "heart" chakra performing at a mediocre level. She suggested Katrina visualize a verdant valley, limes, and lush meadows of clover. As with the other energy centers, once Mary Ellen applied her healing, the heart chakra gained strength. She found the remainder of Katrina's chakras were in order.

Mary Ellen's talent and ability as a Reiki healer were evident. She carried out her tasks with precision and sensitivity. This prolonged session helped set a foundation of mutual admiration and respect. They continued to compare notes on their abilities—one using her psychic ability to see from a distance and to sense energy waves; the other using her mind to heal and to read the spiritual realm that affects life on Earth.

"You know, we get along so well, it's like we belong to the same tribe," quipped the Apache woman. "The tribe here in Dulce is having its Pow Wow in mid-July. They call it Little Beaver Days, for the tourists. They have rodeos and it's a great party for a week. I'd love to have you come out for a couple days. You could stay with me. We could have some good discussions."

Katrina accepted Mary Ellen's offer. Her Jicarilla Apache friend was delighted. The common psychic abilities had allowed them to bond. Mary Ellen recognized Katrina had so much potential as a human, but it had been masked by the negative experiences and influences she had known. She wanted Katrina to understand her abilities better. Both grew excited about their meeting.

19

. . . DULCE

Mary Ellen met Katrina at Albuquerque airport. The three-hour ride back to Dulce didn't seem so long, since they spent it in fully engaged conversation. Mary Ellen explained a little about Little Beaver Days, told her life story and how she became an orphan in Albuquerque, then how she was admitted back into the tribe when she turned sixteen. Katrina told Mary Ellen of her dysfunctional family, her late brother and being with him when he died, and her ailing mother. She also explained her rapid and ill-advised marriage and talked of her daughter, now on the cusp of being an adult.

"The people on the *rez* are not very warm to white people," Mary Ellen said. "Make sure you stay by me. If we do not see my clan tomorrow, I'll introduce them to you at the Pow Wow on Saturday."

They arrived at the Jicarilla Apache Reservation just before dinner. As they headed into Dulce, they drove past the fairgrounds and the Pow Wow circle. The locals were still setting up for the parade, scheduled for the next day. Carnival rides were being assembled, and the food trucks were pulling into their positions.

Katrina turned to Mary Ellen, a warm smile in her eyes and face. "Thanks for inviting me, Mary Ellen. This is probably the most fun I have had in a long time. Already."

"You are the first outsider I've had stay with me. It's so good to have you here. I think you'll enjoy the next couple days."

Mary Ellen pointed out all the main buildings and attractions on their way to her trailer. She then pointed north-northwest. "Over in that direction is Archuleta Mesa. It's the source of a lot of rumor. Some tribes people, mostly the elders, say they have seen craft fly out of the mountain. Ancient legend says our ancestors were assisted by beings that emerged from below the ground. The beings provided the ancients with seeds and tubers, and taught them to hunt for food, clothing, and shelter. They think some kind of beings still live in that mountain."

"Do you believe that too?"

There was silence for a moment before she replied. "I have reason to believe there is something going on in that mountain. Close to the top of the mesa, there are signs restricting access. There is a portion of the mesa that is government land. Some of the land is owned by an energy company. We have heard of trespassers being stopped by the Jicarilla Police. Some folks I trust were able to get close enough to hear sounds coming from underground. Someday, I am going to find out what the truth is."

Mary Ellen's trailer was only about a half-mile north of the fairgrounds at the edge of a residential area. Since the front door faced south, it was the ideal spot to view the nightlife at the festival. Once inside, Mary Ellen prepared a quick casual dinner while Katrina unpacked. Before dinner, Mary Ellen asked Katrina if she wanted to join her in a meditation session. Katrina told Mary Ellen she did not engage in the practice on a regular basis, because of the incident involving Sonny Lyle when she was in college. Mary Ellen listened closely with bewilderment as Katrina described the incident in detail.

"I cannot imagine what that would feel like—being trapped inside someone else's body," Mary Ellen said.

Katrina shook her head. "I was terrified. To this day, I don't know if it was me or him that caused it to happen. I had had only one psychic experience prior to that."

"So, you don't meditate, and yet you have those amazing abilities?" asked Mary Ellen.

"Yes. Does that seem odd to you?"

"Very. First, your abilities are beyond anything I could even try to achieve. I meditate daily, sometimes twice a day. I will never reach your level of activity. You say that you don't have good control over your power. I think you would gain better control and consistency, and have a more grounded approach to life, if you meditated. Meditation activates your pineal gland. It's like opening a present inside you. Trust me, you will feel the benefit after you get into a routine."

Katrina agreed to join Mary Ellen in meditation. They quieted themselves. The session began with disciplined breathing and visualization of good energy entering during the inhale and bad energy exiting during the exhale. Katrina and Mary Ellen finished the exercise. As she entered the meditative state, Katrina received an image of Mount Archuleta. Her perspective took her closer to the mesa on the surface. She recognized the posted No Trespassing signs Mary Ellen described. A field of tall wild grasses grew atop the mesa, sparsely highlighted by not so significant trees. The image faded, to be replaced by a new image appearing to be inside and underground. She sensed a strong energy field, and it attracted her. The energy led her to what appeared to be a hangar bay with exotic aerial vehicles. Looking more closely, she detected nonhuman occupants. They were anthropomorphic creatures with reptilian features. The vision shocked her, and she cut off the meditation with an abrupt vocal intake of air:

"Oh..."

"What happened? What's wrong?" asked Mary Ellen, disturbed by the reaction.

"You said that you would eventually find out the truth about Mount Archuleta?" Katrina asked softly. "I have it for you. The old natives are right. During mediation, I remote-viewed the mesa. I was able to find an energy source where there were UFOs in an underground hangar. The place was populated by tall reptilian creatures. They were hideous, wearing warrior type uniforms, having large sharp claws and menacing-looking teeth."

"I'm not surprised. The old folks who say they saw ships coming from that mountain are very respected in town. I trust them. They wouldn't make up stories like that." Mary Ellen's lack of emotion and surprise did surprise Katrina.

They continued talking through dinner. Mary Ellen brought out a bottle of red wine, and the two women talked as if they were old friends, sharing deeply personal stories of past encounters with men. They could have chatted all night, but Mary Ellen had other plans.

"We had better get to bed. We are going to get up early to see the parade."

* * *

After a restful sleep, both women enjoyed a hasty breakfast and walked to the fairgrounds. On the way, Mary Ellen explained the origin of Little Beaver Days.

"So, the name came from the Red Ryder comic strip that was popular in...I want to say, the 1940s. Little Beaver was the name of the Apache partner to Red Ryder. Sometime in the mid-50s, there was a TV show based on the comic strip. The young actor playing Little Beaver in the TV show came from Dulce. Someone tried to set up a theme park in Albuquerque, named Little Beaver Park. That failed. So, people in Dulce decided to carry on the memory of Little Beaver with the combination Pow Wow and rodeo."

Mary Ellen and Katrina picked a spot under a tree to watch the parade. Each year, the parade had a theme. This year's theme was the superhero. Every vehicle/float carried the theme of a famous comic book hero. The parade was led by Miss Little Beaver on her own float. Mary Ellen and Katrina stayed to the end. The parade watching was followed by sitting in the stands to watch rodeo events such as bull riding, roping, bronco riding, and barrel races. After the rodeo, they walked around the grounds, enjoying the sunny day. Many people walked up to say hello to Mary Ellen, who was a social worker on the reservation. The women sampled the offerings from several food trailers over the course of the afternoon and early evening. The walk home was slow. It was a relaxing end to the day. Mary Ellen and Katrina were satisfied with their day.

* * *

To ensure she would have time to meet her clan prior to the Pow Wow, Mary Ellen and Katrina started their next day early. They made their way to the dirt circle called the walk path. It was surrounded by small, sheet metal, open-air pavilions. Under one of the pavilions, Mary Ellen recognized members of her clan, the Ollero. Everyone got up from their lawn chairs or benches and went to greet and hug their "lost daughter" who had returned years ago. Mary Ellen introduced Katrina as part Cherokee. They politely acknowledged her with a wave or a timid hello.

Mary Ellen explained her clan's history to Katrina. "The women here take the craft of making garments seriously," she said.

"We come from a long line of master dressmakers, bead crafters, and basket weavers," added one of the women.

"A couple of our clan are at the Arts and Craft tent, Mary Ellen," added another woman.

"There are garments displayed in the Wheelwright Museum of the American Indian in Santa Fe, made by Conelia and Lesao Garcia

Velarde—I am a direct descendant," Mary Ellen pointed out, her pride shining in her eyes.

The women were preparing for the dance around the circle, which included a competition for best traditional outfits. Mary Ellen continued to talk to relatives. Katrina took a seat. Mary Ellen noticed and took a bottle of water to her.

"The women need help in getting their outfits together for the circle dance. I won't be long," she assured Katrina.

"I'll be alright, Mary Ellen. Go ahead and do what you need to. I'll watch."

Mary Ellen went back to a circle of women working on their outfits. One of the outfits, the signature garment from the Jicarilla Apache culture, was a poncho. It served as the ceremonial garment to celebrate the coming of age for the Jicarilla women. Officially, it is a cape with unmistakable qualities to distinguish its authenticity. Their cape was made of deerskin, dyed in yellow. The back and front had scalloped edges outlined with six stripes of alternating colors of blue, black, and white. The neck was adorned at the edges with bright, contrasting bead work. It was fringed at the sides, extending beyond arm length. The clan did not stray from the authentic designs and never used a machine to put it together. All authentic garments were made by hand.

Katrina took a drink and leaned back against the chair, looking to Mount Archuleta. Her vision in front of her dissipated ...

She saw UAVs in the mountain. She sensed another energy field, and discovered what appeared to be a laboratory with creatures connected to wire, hoses, and cables that were enveloped in sacs and suspended in tanks of pinkish fluid. Katrina looked closer. The creatures in the tubes appeared to have human physical traits. She moved to another part of that laboratory and witnessed more creatures in the form of younger humans. Her remote view continued to other parts of the lab, witnessing creatures in various stages of development.

The discovery of a laboratory with living creatures in suspension disturbed her greatly. She stopped the viewing activity and took a drink. However, compelled by a sense of duty, she decided she needed to see more. Focusing again, she sensed yet another source of energy coming from another point underground. It was an energy wave familiar to her, a nuclear reactor, much smaller than the one at Rancho Seco. For the first time, she also witnessed humans nearby, manning the controls. On one side of the site, there was a reptilian operation, while on the other, the underground facility was inhabited by humans. Right in Mary Ellen's backyard, there appeared to be a joint operation between a reptilian alien race and humans.

It was the most bizarre series of visions she had ever viewed remotely, downright confusing. Looking closely at the human side of the operation, she could see many people in uniform but no insignia. She detected multiple levels underground, occupied on both sides. This discovery went beyond verifying that the natives were correct about activity underground.

Katrina decided that she had seen enough. She stopped the viewing and she made eye contact with Mary Ellen, who was helping a woman with feathers on a headdress. Mary Ellen sensed something odd about Katrina's expression and walked to her.

"Are you OK?"

"I'll tell you later. Go back to helping your family." Katrina took another drink from her bottle.

Mary Ellen spent more time with her clan as Katrina looked on. It was time for the dance. The women's final step was to fasten the tag displaying their registered number for the judges. Loud beats thumped from the circle as men and boys pounded on their handheld ceremonial drum. Boxy audio speakers were set on a pole in the center to amplify the drums and chants.

The tan, dusty soil made a natural backdrop for the brightly colored vestments. Women strolled around clockwise in a circle, but there were no lanes. The Native American pageantry stood out in its glory against the perfect blue sky and puffs of clouds. Children joined in to walk with the women. The outfits were complete with leather moccasins on their feet. Women wore their long black hair in braids. Beads adorned their outfits. Feathers were bright and long. They strolled around the circle for a number of rounds: a slow kaleidoscope of a rich human vortex.

After the walk path and the judging, Mary Ellen and Katrina visited the other tents. Mary Ellen was able to introduce Katrina to other members of her clan. Katrina looked on as men were demonstrating the traditional technique of basket weaving. A monitor on a table looped a video of men gathering willow and sumac branches. A woman, in the course of weaving, was using a knife and her teeth in an alternating fashion. The craftworkers never strayed from the original technique: no machines. Another video showed how the workers used chokecherries to manufacture a dye to color the basketware, giving it a dull burgundy-red tint. The baskets were in high demand around the world, reflected in prices that reached five figures for a single basket. Mary Ellen explained that the crafts of the Jicarilla Apache were a reflection of a culture of patience, pride, and love.

The two women continued to stroll to other tents. Displayed were beaded bags, moccasins, and more ceremonial ponchos. An adjacent tent displayed another Jicarilla specialty: micaceous pottery. The mica content gave the finish an iridescent quality.

"I love the way it sparkles!" exclaimed Katrina.

"I do too. I have been meaning to get one for myself for some time."

"How about I get you one, and you get me one?" Katrina said. "That way it would be more than just buying it. I get to pick something for you, and you could pick mine."

Katrina picked a bowl with a design fashioned by embedding and coating horse hair. Mary Ellen selected a platter with a raised cross design in the center. They passed a tent sponsored by the local Wild Horse Casino and one where KCIE public radio was broadcasting live reports. The last tent they passed before heading back was another cultural exhibit about learning the true native Abaachi language.

With the afternoon slipping toward evening, Mary Ellen said her goodbyes to her family and friends. She and Katrina headed back to the trailer. It was Katrina's last night, and Mary Ellen wanted to take advantage of her time with Katrina. She had intentions that, if Katrina moved forward with them, would affect her for the rest of her life.

"What was it that upset you today?" Mary Ellen asked.

Katrina was still unsure what she had seen, but she described it to Mary Ellen as best she could.

"The images appeared just as I looked toward the mesa. First, I clearly saw UFOs in line. As you know, I get images from energy waves. I sensed a strong energy beyond those UFOs and saw—well, I don't know what I saw. There are four lab rooms. Each room has a large glass enclosure and behind the enclosure appeared to be humanoid beings in sacs with pinkish liquid or gel in separate larger tubes. Each humanoid connected to tubes and cables and hoses."

"Labs with humans in tubes? In Mount Archuleta?" Mary Ellen's eyebrows arched up her forehead as she motioned to the mesa.

"Yes. I didn't want to look any further into that lab. It was so disturbing. I shifted my view to another part where I sensed a larger amount of concentrated energy. I found a facility powered by a small nuclear reactor, manned by humans, not the reptilian creatures I saw before."

The information brought both clarity and horror to Mary Ellen.

She was still stuck on the previous revelation. "There's a lab, and they are holding humanoid creatures?"

"Yes." Katrina nodded with a concerned look.

"I've heard stories and read blogs about this. So, it's true, then."

Katrina nodded again. "Yes."

"Imagine, something like that happening here, where I see the mountain every day. I have had sensations, disturbances in my meditation. I have had a repeating nightmare, where I could see and hear children screaming. The disturbances are eerily similar in sensation. I am going to think about this information you gave me. It's possible I have been misinterpreting or ignoring something very important."

Mary Ellen thanked Katrina for the information. It validated her feelings about the mountain. Katrina proved to be a valuable friend, and Mary Ellen wanted to show her gratitude.

"Katrina, before you go back to Nevada, I would like to help you spiritually. Would you let me read you? The healing we did yesterday was only a part of what I can do to help you. Something that I can manipulate continues to keep you from reaching the greatest strength in your abilities. Would you let me try something?"

"I've told you about the amount of harassment I withstood. I'm afraid it actually took something away from me," Katrina explained, entirely comfortable with opening up fully to Mary Ellen, as if she'd been a lifelong friend. "Would you be able to tell? Would you be able to help me get it back?"

"Reading you would be like being a mechanic checking a car's engine. I will easily be able to describe the damage and tell you how to repair it. I am amazed by what you can do with your mind. But I think your encounters with those horrible men have cut into your spirit, leaving wounds unique to only you. Your beaten spirit has become accustomed to retaliate violently and indiscriminately. That is why you feel you don't have control. I will focus on your heart chakra again, and if you let me heal you, you will be able to control your ability better, because your heart is essential to your ability."

"What do you mean when you mention my spirit? Are you talking about something related to God? I don't have any belief and I am skeptical of religion. Nothing tells me that we are being guided by some higher power. If we are, he's not doing a good job."

"I understand how you feel," Mary Ellen said, taking Katrina's hand, cupping it, relaxing her. "Both sides of the discussion are partially correct. The truth is somewhere between atheism and religion. Atheists, like you, should understand there are higher energies that guide us. They are energies we cannot see or touch. They exist in another realm. The religious people need to understand those energies can be explained through science. Neither belief is completely accurate. What we call 'God' cannot exist through spirituality or science alone."

Mary Ellen explained the Source energy and how it relates to human spirituality. She described the spiritual realm and how humans are able to reach that realm through meditation and in dreams. Katrina listened intently. Mary Ellen sat directly across from Katrina, so she could look at her as she communicated to her what transpired.

"It is just as I described. Your heart chakra is not balanced. Holding a grudge consumes the essence of your being a loving, caring, forgiving human. Before I work on you again, you need to hear this. If you want to have control over your abilities, you will have to have control of your spirituality. You must recognize you can be greater than the ones that attacked you, only if you choose NOT to be like them. You have to reach higher in spirit. Only then, will you be balanced, keeping control of yourself and your greater power over those that want to damage you. Katrina, listen to me. You are NOT like them. You are greater than they could ever imagine to be. Your gift is immeasurable and your abilities are as well."

This was exactly the opposite guidance she had received from DD. Katrina felt conflicted. "What do you want me to do?" she asked. "I was told I was able to fight back because I decided to be like them. They told me I would die if I did not retaliate."

"I'm not telling you not to retaliate. I am telling you that you shouldn't do it without emotion or understanding of what you are doing to the person you are fighting. Your thoughts and intentions have long-term and deep effects on your ability. I am going to ask you a simple test question. Answer it honestly and clearly."

Katrina nodded. "Okay..."

"How do you feel when you see an animal on the road that had been hit by a car?"

Without pause, Katrina replied. "I feel horrible, empty. I want to care for it."

"See? You are not completely void of kindness. Katrina, you are not 'them.' You don't want to be like 'them,' always living in a dark and pessimistic world of fear. I live in a world of love, peace, togetherness. You are destined to be that way too. Be proud of who you are and embrace it. Celebrate it, like I celebrate my Apache blood. It is time for you to repair. Be kind to yourself. Do something nice for yourself, and then tell yourself you are a good person for others. I can't ask you to show your love for everyone until you love yourself."

Katrina silently nodded to acknowledge Mary Ellen's teachings.

"Everyone here on this planet has a unique and amazing spirit connected to them. Imagine that. We are more than just humans with bones, blood, and organs. We all have our own special spirit. Each spirit has an assignment here. We are not allowed to end that assignment until we learn our lessons—whatever they may be. Each and every one of us are here to help others through their assignments. The assignment must be held sacred, so life is sacred. Imagine how we would treat each other if we held to that fact. Katrina: We must respect the lives we touch. For every life you show kindness and love, you will gain spiritual strength, and in your case, it will affect your electromagnetics. Your ability is not only dependent upon your magnificent mind. It is also dependent upon your heart. With this understanding, you will be a formidable opponent to those who attack you."

Katrina sat silently and nodded solemnly, accepting every word.

"Remember, your existence and your spirit combine to make a wonderful human. We are all wonderful that way."

Mary Ellen instructed Katrina to join her in meditation for a while. They both sat silently, concentrating on the breath entering and exiting the body. It was a peaceful and restful session for both. Katrina did not remote view. She concentrated on her own existence, and she liked what she felt.

After their meditation concluded, Mary Ellen went to the kitchen to fix something simple: stove-warmed fresh tortillas, chorizo, avocado, and fresh tomatoes from her garden. Katrina went to pack up. They sat out on the deck at the front of the trailer and watched the fireworks marking the end of Little Beaver Days and the end of their time together... for now.

20

. . . A MUTUAL RESCUE

The veteran's rough life made him look older than he was. Getting used to the absence of warmth at night, he imagined being in the mountains of Afghanistan. After a long day of panhandling, he surrendered his will and some of his day's earning to a half-pint. It was his way to self-medicate, at the risk of corrupting his body and mind. The addiction diminished his spirit, deconstructing him from a hero to an anonymous lost soul.

He roamed the city without destination, avoiding as much personal contact as possible, aside from his fundraising come-ons. Stumbling, he stopped to rest, still haunted by scrambled thoughts and unbearable memories. He curled with his back to the wind and lay down on his worn but reliable backpack, the thoughts of his past always with him. After faithfully serving two tours in Iraq, then two more in Afghanistan as a senior NCO Army Ranger, he was later diagnosed with PTSD, honorably discharged, and discarded. Like many, he was a victim of a society without conscience, where self-appointed "patriots" who never served waved their assorted flags in hypocrisy. He was on the social back burner where people chanting "America First" continued their jingoistic fervor. It was a shallow nationalism supported by those who worked to weaken the very institutions that were set up to rescue veterans like himself from a gradual decline into useless anonymity.

His illness and addiction made it difficult to hold a job. He disliked going to the Veteran's Administration hospital, where he witnessed health-care workers being overtaxed and treated poorly. His first and last visit forced him to look into the eyes of men and women who were once robust and vibrant defenders of freedom, reduced to the needy and neglected. In the field, doctors were quick to prescribe addictive opioids. The practice continued when he returned to the states. The veteran successfully avoided getting snared into the trap that so many thousands succumbed to. He preferred his occasional episode of PTSD to being dependent on the drug and the broken system.

Being homeless brought him the familiarity of survival. He was comfortable not being comfortable. It was similar to what he had to do in the field while on patrols off base in the mountains of Southwest Asia. He did not know what the following day would bring, but that did not distress him. On this particular night, he had no way of knowing that his life would change drastically . . .

* * *

After several years without any unwelcome interruptions, Katrina left NASA and went back to work in the engineering field. Emma was accepted to the Orvis School of Nursing at the University of Nevada, Reno, about an hour away from Fernley. Katrina would live by herself, in her used trailer on the east side of town, after she helped her daughter move in to her dorm at Juniper Hall.

Once Emma was done unpacking, Katrina took her out to dinner. They talked about what the school year would bring. Katrina described her days at San Diego State, omitting any mention of the episode in the Chi studio. After dinner, Katrina drove her daughter back to the dorm, said her goodbyes, and left for home. Her route home took her on a detour that routed her through construction. Before long, she felt her front passenger tire flopping. She drove her hobbled vehicle to a vacant parking lot. She exited the car, hearing only the clicks of the nearby relay box for the traffic signal. She parked under a security light mounted on an old closed-up building. It provided adequate illumination to accomplish her task. Katrina did not lack the know-how to change a tire, so panic didn't set in. No one would have to be called out of bed to drive to Reno to assist her.

Katrina systematically proceeded to loosen the lugs. As she did, two men appeared out of a nearby alley, their obscene banter amplified by the overconsumption of alcohol. Out of the corner of her eye, Katrina kept a watch on their movement. She was stuck. The old tire was still on the wheel. Noticing her alone and helpless, the men walked directly toward her. The closer they got, the lewder and more graphic their language. Aside from her and the drunken derelicts, the city was a barren place of darkness and stillness. She decided not to acknowledge them, continuing to work on her tire.

As they arrived, one of the men lunged and grabbed the tire iron out of her hands, tossing it across the lot. It banged the pavement, making a loud clanging sound that ripped through the night's stillness. The other man grabbed Katrina by the arm and pulled her up lasciviously, his mouth going on and on with descriptions of their depraved intent. Katrina reacted with screams and uncontrolled kicks as the men began to assault her.

Her screams alerted the nearby homeless vet, hours into his sheltered sleep. His drunkenness nearly worn off, he slowly rolled, knocking over his empty bottle. He sprung to all fours and emerged from his temporary alcohol-induced hibernation. The screams did not stop. He got up and ambled toward the source. As he neared, he could detect the sound of a woman struggling and thrashing violently, accompanied by the raging yells of two men expressing a desire to dominate her. Getting closer, he focused and was finally able to visually distinguish the three people. The woman appeared to be making every effort to resist.

"You men should stop what you are doing now and leave," the unkempt urban nomad demanded.

The two men stopped and were puzzled, as they caught sight of the source of the command. "Look. It's Batman! Hey, Batman, you don't look so good," the first attacker jeered.

The second attacker laughed. "No. It's a wino, and he wants us to stop."

The man tightened his hold on Katrina, pulling on her hair, and turned her head toward the stranger. His partner laughed hard enough to end in a wretched cough, but he still held her, keeping her arms still and pinned to her sides. Katrina was repulsed, and the sight of the homeless man, standing with a slight lurch, trying to stop the crime, appeared to be more a sick joke than a rescue.

The broken, rumpled stranger continued to walk slowly, sauntering, toward the scene. His raspy voice struggled to broadcast another warning. Katrina's attacker let go of her hair, annoyed by the interruption. He began to walk menacingly toward the stranger. This time the untidy bum straightened his posture, trying to appear more alert and even more threatening. The assailant took out a knife from his coat and charged at his target, cutting into his jacket and slicing a wound just above the hip. Shocked, the stranger reacted with a yelp and cussed his apparent decline in speed and agility.

"Pain is the departure of weakness from the body," he remembered. And it came back to him: hand to hand combat training and prior experiences with the bad guys.

The assailant looked at his wounded victim, ambivalent to the injury. Blood oozed from his side and traced down his leg, but he offered no sign of pain. Without warning, in what appeared to be an unrealistic quickness, the stranger surprised his attacker with a leap and a hard solid kick on the man's chin, stunning him. The reinvigorated homeless man finished his attacker with a solid punch in the solar plexus, damaging ribs, causing the man to collapse to the pavement in pain.

The defeat of his partner and the manner in which he was dispatched was unexpected for the man gripping Katrina. In a panic, he produced his own knife and held it under Katrina's chin, threatening to kill her if the stranger attempted to get closer. He began to drag her away as the wounded but tenacious stranger followed. Katrina realized she needed to retaliate in her own way if she were to live through the assault. Her attacker hustled her away from her car, toward the alley. Passing a pole, she noticed two transformers installed above them. She quickly sensed the energy in both, welcoming the invading waves, inviting them to caress her mind. A strange, comforting infusion began to build. Her spine began the familiar anticipated tingle. Sensing she was approaching capacity, she reversed it back in a single burst. The jolt caused the equipment to spark then explode in violent shooting flames. The commotion was enough to distract her assailant, allowing her to escape his grasp. Recalling lessons in personal defense, she quickly spun around and thrust her knee hard up into his groin, then she grabbed the wrist of the hand holding the knife and jerked it down, causing it to stab his leg. The attacker fell forward to the pavement, screaming in agony. Reacting to the explosions, Katrina's rescuer shrieked and dropped to the ground, shielding his head with both hands in a fetal position.

Katrina surveyed the scene. The first assailant sprawled on the pavement, writhing in pain. The stranger was also on the pavement, motionless, face down, still with his hands on his head. The second assailant stood directly behind her, holding his bleeding leg and whimpering. Seeing the knife off to the side, she went to kick it away toward the curb. She then retrieved her tire iron, walked back to her Jeep, and approached the first assailant. Holding the iron over his head as a threat, she commanded him to get up and leave, "And take your partner with you!" The man got up, struggled to his fallen accomplice, and together, they hobbled down the alley.

With her attackers gone, Katrina walked to the stranger, who curled up in his original position, petrified. She stood over the man, then bent down to look at him. Sensing her presence, he turned to look up at her. He appeared confused, his face contorted from the rush of fear. He had no life in his eyes; he wasn't looking at anything in particular. Then he glanced up at the smoldering pair of transformers in a stupor.

Katrina broke his trance. "Thank you for coming to my aid. Are you alright?"

The stranger shifted to a more upright sitting posture. Katrina made an ominous discovery. The left side of his coat was soaked from his blood. The stranger didn't appear concerned.

"You are bleeding!"

"I'll be fine," he replied weakly, with a low voice.

"We need to find you medical attention."

"No. The VA is already packed. Don't take me there."

"You're a veteran?"

"Yeah—Iraq and Afghanistan—I left in early 2008." He rushed through the words, tired of having to explain himself. "I mean it. Don't take me to the VA. Besides, it's not serious. I just need some bandages and rest." Then he lamented, cussing again, that the assailants disturbed his sleep.

Katrina paused. The wound appeared serious enough to her. "I live about an hour east in Fernley. You could come with me. You could rest and get fixed up there. What's your name?"

"Robert Ladd."

"My name is Katrina Hermann."

"What the hell happened? I was just about to help you when there was an explosion right over my head. Didn't that scare you?" Robert asked.

"No."

Robert shook his head and looked down. *How bad am I that this woman did not have a reaction to the blasts while I dropped to the ground like I was under attack?*

"Look, um ... Katrina. ... The war damaged me. I have PTSD. The VA wants to give me drugs, but I don't want to be an addict like other vets that have PTSD. I found drinking to be more manageable—for me."

Robert got up and walked to her Jeep. Katrina followed and resumed changing her tire. Robert shed his bloodied jacket, retrieved a knife, and ripped up the garment into strips of cloth to dress his wound.

Katrina felt it was the right time to confess as Robert trained his attention to treating his injury. "I caused that explosion to distract my attacker. I had self-defense classes when I was younger. He was drunk. He wasn't much of a challenge after I got the advantage."

Robert stopped the knife in mid-cut. "You caused the explosion?"

Katrina paused briefly. "Yes. I am psychokinetic. I detect energy in space like SONAR detects objects in water. I am able to direct my own electromagnetic brain waves to the energies and reverse them. I can cause electrical equipment to heat up quickly. The transformers overheated and exploded."

After Katrina was done explaining, Robert resumed cutting the cloth. "I heard about psychic people, but not like you."

* * *

"Wait, Mom. You told me you and Robert met at a Fourth of July parade. You told me he was reformed alcoholic when you met him."

"I was protecting him, darling. Now you know how we really met. He saved me. I think he was always a good person. He was damaged by the war."

"Well. . . . It's not like I see him a lot. When I *do* see him, he keeps to himself."

"He's getting better with other people."

* * *

Robert worked on his dressing while Katrina continued to explain her ability. He watched her change the tire efficiently. He did not have time to sit long for a break. Katrina was wrapping up and looked over to him as he remained in silent admiration of this woman.

"Are you going to get in the car, soldier?" she asked almost coyly.

Robert opened the door, looking over the roof at Katrina, and saw her smile at him. He hadn't felt good about his situation since he could remember. It was strange but welcome. Sitting in the Jeep, Robert resumed his interrupted nap.

Katrina was exhausted by the time she neared home. Robert stirred with the sound of the tires on the gravel, another conditioning element from wartime. The Jeep turned onto the pad that served her modest but fully functional trailer.

Exiting the Jeep, Robert looked up to witness the majesty of the Milky Way. "Looking up at the stars should be one of my better memories from the Afghan hills. We were able to see this... almost heavenly haze of stardust down to the horizon."

Robert paused to remember more. "When I was young, at home in west Texas, I would look to the night skies and think about God and all the people on Earth—how we all look up to the same sky. Now, when I look up and see this, I have thoughts and memories not from home but another place. Night skies in the Afghan hills were always followed by a morning that would take one or two or three guys from us, who would not be able to see that night sky again. Somewhere, right now, there is someone who also won't see this sky tomorrow."

Robert looked at Katrina, who spotted something special in Robert's face, something beyond the limited or hopeless province of a homeless man. "Don't let what happened in Afghanistan change your happy memories. You will always have the power to choose how you look at life. You can remain in your darkness, or you can decide to be the person you were before the war."

Robert didn't reply but looked up at the stars again, adding another memory.

Katrina opened the door to her trailer and directed Robert to the bathroom so he could get out of his ragged old clothes. She collected his rags and deposited them in the washer. Katrina realized she had left the tub filled with water. She knocked on the door.

"You can drain the water from the tub. When you are done in there I can dress your wound properly."

Robert sat on the edge of the tub with both legs in, keeping his dressing dry. Katrina offered her daughter's room for the night. She knocked again, opened the door a crack, and sneaked in a towel as Robert was getting out. He asked Katrina for his backpack. She gathered it and slipped it in.

Robert was grateful to her for her generosity. Still on the other side of the door, Katrina explained where Robert could find the other things he might need.

Katrina waited in the kitchen. He came out, clean, shaven, and wearing fresh clothes from his backpack. He had dressed his wound himself using gauze and bandages he found in the bathroom. All things considered, Robert was pretty easy on the eyes. "There's some hot water if you want tea. You are probably hungry. I have some frozen burritos you can heat up, there's bread and lunchmeat too. Ramen is in that cupboard," she said, pointing.

"Thanks, I'll make a sandwich. I'll have some herbal tea too."

Katrina wanted to stay up and chat with her house guest but needed rest more than conversation. Robert finished his snack and fell asleep easily. Before going to bed, Katrina returned to the bathroom to fill the tub with cold water and ice.

When Katrina got up in the morning, Robert was out of bed. He wasn't to be found in the trailer. Concerned, she looked outside. The Jeep was still there. Katrina opened the door and found Robert sitting on the front deck looking out toward the rising sun. He was in the clothes he had worn to bed.

Robert looked up at her. "Good morning, Katrina. It's nice out here: quiet, and the air is so clean."

"Good morning. *You* are quiet too. I didn't hear you get up. I'm going inside to cook some eggs and bacon. We'll eat here."

"That sounds great! Thanks."

Katrina went back inside to prepare breakfast. Robert followed close behind and offered a hand. She appreciated the gesture, so much so that she cooked his eggs to order and carried the tray of food outside. Robert followed with the coffee and mugs. They both enjoyed the company. Between bites, he remarked about the many things that made it nice to sleep there. He slept well—better than any time he could recall. Robert finished, leaving nothing on his plate. Katrina nursed her coffee while he finished his second cup, straight black.

"Do you have drought problems?" he asked.

"No, the water is for me. I take ice baths to relieve the side effects from my psychokinetic ability."

Robert steered away from further discussion on the topic. Instead, he confided how alcohol, instead of the economy, had made him lose his job. His last drink was yesterday, before falling asleep in the alley. "I avoided being one type of addict, so I wound up an addict of a different kind," he said, talking aimlessly, feeling comfortable speaking to this woman. "I started drinking to sleep better. I started drinking more for my headaches. I'm so far from normal. Normal was a decade ago, before Iraq and Afghanistan. Every time I start to talk about it, I get nervous, anxious, short of breath. A drink makes that go away."

"You want help? It's not going to be from another drink."

Silence.

Katrina left him in the kitchen as she took his clothes out of the dryer to her basket and carried them to the couch to fold them. "I know our county deputy sheriff well. She could help you find a job in town. You can stay here as long as you stay sober. I will be on the watch. I think it's a good deal for you. You could eventually build some savings to get out on your own."

"I have been through many fire fights, ambushes, and IED detonations. None of those challenges compares to my struggle with alcohol. But I never before met anyone that gave a damn. You seem to be sincere. I'll try to give it a better effort."

She smiled. "You saved me last night. Now it's my turn to do the saving."

He nodded, looking down at the floor.

"One more thing," she added. "I meet a lot of interesting people on my blog. One follower informed me that cannabis oil is effective in treating symptoms of PTSD. I sent her a message so I could purchase it from her. She lives near my parents in California. The next time I go out there, I'll pick some up for you."

Robert found work at an auto repair shop. He didn't need any help from Katrina's friends, at least, it didn't appear that way. Katrina began dropping him off at the repair shop on her way to her job at the engineering design firm in Reno.

Robert adjusted to the sober life better than he thought he would. He didn't need any encouragement. Katrina was a gracious host. She never kept any alcohol in the house. Robert took the simple pleasure of enjoying the views, the sunrises, and the sunsets from the trailer. Katrina was happy to have someone to talk to. She learned a lot from Robert's confessions of the days and nights in Southwest Asia. It also gave her an opportunity to reveal her own uniqueness, explaining the harassment and torture, her days at Sierra Remote Viewing, and her own conflicts with Al-Qaeda. Both revealed enough about each other to build a strong trusting relationship. Katrina began to feel affection for Robert, and Robert realized that she was a special woman.

Robert and Katrina went about their daily work routines. Robert had been working on cars, doing very well. The management, impressed with his professional demeanor, thought he exhibited leadership potential. Robert was prompt, courteous to customers, accurately diagnosed problems, and used his time efficiently. His supervisor had no reason to expect problems.

Then one day, an engine backfired outside the shop. It was loud, sudden, and unexpected. Robert, who working under the hood of a car, dropped a tool, backed away, yelled an obscenity, clutched his head and dropped to the ground. Mechanics in the bay turned in disbelief to see him curled up in a ball. A customer saw the incident, which made her uncomfortable. Robert's supervisor rushed over and crouched down next to him to talk to him. Robert looked up, realized he was not in danger, and sheepishly apologized. He looked around the auto shop. His coworkers continued to stare at him. The supervisor decided it would be best if Robert took the rest of the day off. Robert called Katrina, and Katrina left work to pick him up.

"We are going this weekend to get you the CBD oil from my friend in California," Katrina told him as he got in the Jeep. Robert was embarrassed. He wanted a drink. He was fidgety and anxious, consumed with the idea of drinking.

As they approached her gravel road, they saw a white pickup parked opposite her trailer. The taillights turned on and the truck immediately swung left, making a U-turn. It passed her on the opposite side of the road. Robert was startled back to the present. He saw the truck as it passed, its windows darkened to obscure the interior. He recognized this as an imminent threat to the woman who had taken him in and helped him recover. Now he found himself able to take control of the situation and assess the danger. He already had a plan.

"Someone appears to be staking out your trailer, Katrina. If we had not come home early, we wouldn't have known it. It's a late model Nissan. You should call your deputy sheriff friend and let her know that you are being watched."

"I'm not surprised. There are plenty of people from my past who might want revenge. I can handle electromagnetic warfare, but I would be useless against real bullets."

"We need to be alert. Now that they know we suspect something; they will plan to come at you hard. We need to go to town and pick up some guns."

"We don't have to do that. My dad has a small collection. He didn't do much with us as kids, but one thing we did together was go to the range. The day after tomorrow, Saturday, we'll go to my parents' house after picking up the CBD oil."

The incident served as effective distraction. Robert's nerves calmed. His need for a drink also disappeared. Katrina was relieved to have Robert living with her in light of this development.

Robert demonstrated a keen focus on the situation and concern without panic. "We are at a slight disadvantage because we don't know who the adversary is or what they want," he explained. "At least we know there is a threat, a real threat. The sooner we get armed and prepared, the more confident I will feel about this."

Perhaps it was how Robert handled the event. Perhaps it was the way he spoke to her. He made her feel safe. Katrina's attraction to him became deeper and stronger. She stepped closer toward him.

"Robert, you bounced back from your episode today. I'm glad you are here with me." She whispered, "I have all the confidence that you know what to do."

He turned his head toward her, and she looked into his eyes. They leaned toward each other, and their lips met. He felt her warmth, her softness, her delicate breath. She was pleased by his reception, his sturdiness. She stirred his masculine desire.

She broke the kiss. "You aren't sleeping in Emma's room anymore," she said, her words as much a command as a request.

She took his hand and led him to her room. It had been a long time for both.

21

... THE CONTRACT

Katrina and Robert drove west to Sacramento to pick up a few vials of CBD oil from her friend. Each bottle had an eyedropper for dispensing. The woman instructed Robert to place a couple drops under his tongue at the start of an anxiety attack.

From there, they drove to Grass Valley. Katrina ordered lunch and picked it up before returning to her family home. Not much had changed since she had left. Her father was still rather insensitive to Katrina's mother, while her mother's deteriorating health put even greater demands on her in-home care.

Commander Hermann greeted Robert indifferently, with a brief impersonal handshake. Katrina and Robert did not volunteer details about how they met. He had asked Katrina not to tell her father that he was a vet too, preferring not to bring up the wars. Aside from the lunch together, there was little pleasant about the visit. Katrina couldn't wait to leave, but she had an objective to fulfill before departing.

"Dad, you once told me I could have a couple of your guns if I needed them. Well, Dad, I need them. I'd like to take them back with me to my trailer. We have coyotes and they roam in packs. They scare the heck out of me."

Hesitatingly, he obliged, slowly getting up and leading her and Robert to his study where he kept a large armored cabinet. He allowed them to view his collection. He had not purchased a weapon since Katrina left home. Rifles were hung, pistols were in drawers, separated from magazines, with rounds in another drawer.

Robert did not want to appear too knowledgeable, as it would give away his military past. Especially with a Naval commander in the room. He scanned the rifles, looking for a semi-automatic weapon. There were three to choose from. He suggested Katrina take an older version of the AR-15: an M-16. Katrina preferred a pistol and opted for a 9 mm Beretta that she had shot as an older teen. Her father had no objections to letting her take both weapons, and he provided necessary rounds of ammunition and accessories.

"Thanks, Dad. This will really help," she said, keeping it simple and to the point.

The old man immediately closed his cabinet and locked it. Robert took the M-16 and inspected it briskly. The weapon was immaculate. It felt natural, like an extension of his arm. The smooth finish against his palm was a calming feel. His right hand closed over the grip, and the muscle memory provided an odd feeling of security.

Katrina's father took note of Robert's actions. "I see you are familiar with the M-16," he said, locking right in on Robert's handling of the weapon, his ease and comfort with it.

"I have handled it before...a while back."

Katrina deflected the direction of the conversation. She motioned to her father. "Dad, can you show me how to check this pistol? It's been a long time."

Edwin was happy to take the role of small arms instructor for his daughter—again. He took the pistol from her hand and explained each step in detail from removing the cartridge to separating the slide from the frame. Robert went to the car to get a vial of the CBD and placed a drop under his tongue, happy to avoid a confrontation with the commander. Katrina and her father were still deep into the dismantling of her new weapon when Robert returned.

"Why do you need the guns *now*? You've been in that trailer for years. You've always had coyotes. You don't need them for coyotes, do you?" Her father was still sharp.

"And you," he directed his statement to Robert. "You don't need to tell me any more about yourself if you don't want to, son. I worked alongside the finest SEALs and Rangers. I've watched them during exercises. I've observed how they handle their weapons, like a part of themselves. The way you handled that M-16 betrayed your desire to conceal yourself."

So much for playing charades with a seasoned commander.

"US Army Seventy-Fifth Regiment. I served two tours each in Iraq and Afghanistan. How about you, Commander?"

"Naval Intelligence Special Access Programs. That's all I could tell you, son."

"SAP? I had brief encounters with guys in the Air Force—Ground Combat Support. They never smiled."

"That's because they know. They know the truth. They know everything the papers didn't tell you, and like me, they have to keep to themselves until they die—and it eats at you. Ever have anything eat at you, son? I'm sure you saw things that is the stuff of nightmares even for the bravest soldier."

"Yes sir—and like you, I'd rather not talk about it."

"Fair enough, son."

"Robert, sir."

"I retired with the rank of commander."

"Robert, Commander."

Katrina sat listening to Robert and her father's conversation. Her father revealed a human side of compassion and empathy. She wondered why he couldn't extend his comradery to his own family.

"Katrina, if you are in trouble, I can get help for you."

"I don't know who they are, Dad."

Robert added, "Commander, whoever it is has been staking out her trailer. If they wanted to cause damage, they could have easily done it. They want her. They didn't seem like pros, more like hired thugs."

"You saw them?" Edwin asked.

"We saw their vehicle parked as we returned early from work a couple days ago. I think we'll be able to handle them."

Katrina's father nodded. Katrina thanked him and gave him a gentle hug. She went to her mother's room to see her before she left.

Resting almost upright in her bed, her mother's eyes were open, vacant. There was no expression as Katrina walked into her line of sight. She didn't even turn her head. Katrina wondered how much her mother was able to process. Although it was not Katrina's first time to see her that way, she felt her mother had slipped further away. Katrina touched her mother's hand. She looked at the machines, numbers, flashing lights, the sound of a pump, the whir of a small cooling fan. Everything appeared as normal as one would expect. The IV drip took away the pain. Another extended her life.

She turned her head toward Katrina. The Alzheimer's had progressed to the severe stage. Katrina didn't say a word. She smiled at her mother and thought she saw her mother's facial muscles attempt to smile back. It hurt her to think of the life of coldness suffered at the hands of her father. Her mother did not deserve this emotional

... THE CONTRACT

torture. Now she couldn't express herself any more than with just the movement on her face and her lit eyes. Katrina wished she had Mary Ellen's ability to read the mind and spirit. She felt helpless as she cherished her mother's touch. She wasn't sure if anything she could say beyond what she had already told her would be comprehended. She never wanted any of her visits to be the last. This did not feel like the others.

Katrina finally let go. She moved to kiss her mother's forehead, whispered a daughter's love and admiration in her ear, and turned around to leave.

She entered the living room where Robert sat alone, waiting. The guns and accessories were in the Jeep. Robert said her father had retired to his study. Katrina went to tell her father they were leaving, and she thanked him for letting them borrow his guns. He acknowledged her with a nod.

Katrina looked at Robert, not proud of the moment. Robert gave her a look of understanding. In the Jeep, Katrina elaborated on the dysfunction in her family: the insensitive patriarch; the overworked, underappreciated, and dominated housewife; and the sternly raised children. Robert painted a gloomy picture of his family, too. Neither parent coped well with his doing the multiple tours in Southwest Asia. It put a strain on the family. He stayed with the Army because he didn't know what else he could do. After the first tour, he was lost being stateside. He relished the risks and was addicted to the uncertainty, danger, excitement in the extreme. It was a stimulating adventure. He volunteered for more tours. When he finally returned with a medical discharge, his parents blamed him for his injury. He lived with them for a while in rural Texas, but he was out of control and they asked him to leave.

Robert moved to western Nevada to join another veteran from one of his tours. His friend also suffered from PTSD but relied on the medication prescribed by a doctor at the VA hospital in Reno. Together, they worked as hired hands for ranchers. During the fracking boom, they labored at the natural gas wells. Robert's friend became addicted to drugs. Witnessing the grip the drugs had on his friend, he insisted on staying away from the VA. His fear for his friend was realized when he arrived at the shared apartment, walked into the bathroom, and saw his friend's lifeless body on the floor, with a needle by his side. The loss of his friend was one too many losses. He couldn't hold his job and drank to excess, which eventually pushed him onto the streets in Reno. He spent a little more than two years as a faceless, homeless person in the city.

Living with Katrina in her modest trailer felt more like home than anywhere else since leaving his family in Texas. Alone until they found each other, they both realized their relationship was meant to be.

* * *

At night, Katrina lay in bed, curled toward the door. Robert slept on the window side. The window stayed opened slightly, to keep the room cool for Katrina. From his time sleeping in the open and hostile parts of the theater of operation, Robert learned to sleep aware, the slightest sounds awakening him. Like tires. Tires on gravel make an unmistakable sound, especially when disturbing the silence of the desert night.

Robert heard a vehicle approach along Katrina's gravel road. He looked out the window and saw a vehicle drawing nearer with only its parking lights on. His instinct alerted him to an imminent threat. He shoved Katrina awake.

"We have company! Get up. Get your sneakers on and get out quickly! We need to get to the crawlspace—now!"

Katrina sat up swiftly, jumped out, grabbed her phone, threw on a sweatshirt, and slipped on her unlaced sneakers. Robert reached for his vial, backpack, her pistol, and his newly acquired M-16 as the truck turned to the trailer's gravel pad. Slipping on his shoes, he rushed to the kitchen, managing to get a drop of the CBD.

Not completely dressed, they flipped the trapdoor in the floor open. Robert stayed low as Katrina scurried down the opening. He hopped down next as he heard the truck stop and doors open. A barrage of automatic gunfire erupted. The trailer was riddled, bullets crashing glass and anything within range in the space above them. Katrina lay as low as possible on the dusty ground, frozen in terror by the constant gunfire ravaging her home and everything inside it.

* * *

"Now, this I knew. Everyone knew. It was all over town, but I don't remember hearing it on the news."

"Yeah. The town operated differently, and having Lisa as a friend helped in keeping things quiet in the media."

"When I learned about it, a lot of time passed, and it wasn't from you or Grandpa. I think I know why you didn't tell me right away."

"You were still in school. I saw nothing good in scaring you unnecessarily."

* * *

Robert crawled to the front to look through the lattice skirt. He recognized the truck as the one they encountered the previous week. He spied four men: two men on each side of the truck, each equipped with a military-style assault rifle. Robert scrambled to the back corner of the trailer and as the gunfire continued, he forced himself out through a joint in the lattice. He positioned himself at the rear corner of the trailer, in line with the two men standing on the passenger side. He waited for the gunfire to stop, making sure all rounds were expended. The firing stopped as the four men admired their destruction. Assured they were done, Robert aimed and fired two deadly shots at the men, hitting both in the chest. The bullets entered with such a high velocity that the force caused a damaging suction as the projectile shot through each assailant's body. They exited through much larger holes than the one they made upon entry, as the bullets ravaged the men's insides, pulling away chunks of vital internal organs and blood.

The other two shooters rushed back to the truck. Immediately, the driver gunned the engine. Robert got up and fired more rounds into the vehicle, through the glass, on the driver's side, shattering the windshield. Robert watched as the truck began to roll in reverse toward the edge of a shallow ravine. Not stopping, the back dropped down as Robert watched the front end raise up and begin to slide, disappearing from view. Robert ran to watch it at the edge and see it go down, then turn and roll a few times, coming to a rest upside down in the brush.

Katrina emerged from under the trailer, shaken and scared. Acrid smoke from the gunfire lingered over the scene. The night was still again as she walked timidly toward the dead men on her gravel pad, lying among their emptied guns and casings. She glanced back at Robert as he looked down on the wreck. The darkness made it difficult to see any detail. He was able to hear a voice moan for help, evidently in distress. Katrina went to her Jeep to get a flashlight and handed it to Robert. He used it as he scaled down the slope to reach the truck, about thirty feet down. The lone survivor in the truck continued to call out, noticeably in pain.

Robert arrived at the inverted truck, its cab roof partially crushed. Robert saw the man was lying flat against the roof, his limbs limp, not moving. A bullet wound in his left shoulder stained his shirt. The driver had probably died from shots in the upper chest, but he had been thrown around the cab of the truck. His head was turned and wedged in a grisly fashion against the shattered windshield, spattered from his own blood.

Robert held his weapon, aimed at the survivor. The man lay still, in fear.

"Who hired you to do this to Katrina?" Robert demanded.

The man shook his head. "Don't shoot, please." His accent was all too familiar, carrying Robert back to his deployments.

"I am only going to ask you one more time, who hired you?"

"We take orders from Ali," the injured assailant said, his voice little more than a wisp.

Katrina placed a call to her deputy sheriff friend.

"Katrina! What time is it? Are you in trouble?"

"Lisa!"

"What? Are you alright?" The deputy began to stir and got out of bed.

"I'm OK. My trailer is all shot up. I . . ."

"What? Where are the shooters? Did you see them? Are they still at large?"

"Robert killed two. There were four. The two other guys tried to escape. Robert shot at them, and the truck backed into the ravine and rolled. Robert is at the crash site now. I am standing right over the bodies of the two men he shot. It was the truck that Robert and I caught staking us out."

"Are you OK?"

"I'm not hurt, I'm still shaking."

"Alright. Do not call anyone else. Don't call 911. I'll be right there."

They ended the call.

Robert recalled the name Ali from one of Katrina's stories. Surveying the truck and its immobile occupants, and not seeing any other weapons, he determined there was no threat from the survivor, and he started to ascend the slope.

Katrina met him at the edge.

"They work for your old friend, Ali," Robert said.

She was not surprised. Though years had passed, she had anticipated trouble from her old nemesis at some time. However, she expected an attack from an energy weapon, not four assailants rolling up in a truck and blasting her home to smithereens. She was beyond angry that he had tried to kill her this way. *Coward!* she thought.

She turned back to look at her trailer more closely. She saw bullets holes, broken glass, curtains waving in the wind through the opening. They walked back to the trailer. The front door was shot up. Robert managed to open it. They stepped in and surveyed the scene with the flashlight. Broken glass was everywhere. The power was out. Shots had hit the fuse box. They heard water leaking. Rounds had hit the pipes as well. Robert took his and Katrina's guns back to her Jeep.

It didn't take long for Deputy Sheriff Lisa to arrive in near silence. Katrina greeted her immediately, pointing to the trailer and the bodies. Before exiting her squad car, she directed lights to the scene. Katrina continued talking to her as she walked toward the bodies. Looking at Robert, standing next to Katrina, she asked him what had happened, and Robert replied, even though Katrina was telling her what happened from the moment Lisa got out of her car. She looked closely at the bodies and the weapons that lay, untouched, beside the men. Robert mentioned the wreck in the ravine and the two men.

"There's a survivor?" she asked.

"Yes. He's in bad shape, but he'll live."

"That makes things a little messier." The deputy sheriff looked around. "Where is the weapon you used to shoot?"

"We had two weapons. Robert discharged only one. My father lent them to us," Katrina replied. "They are in my Jeep."

Lisa did not respond. As long as there was legal possession, and the gun was clearly used in self-defense, there was no need to take the guns away; at least, she felt it wasn't necessary.

The deputy sheriff got on the radio and requested a forensic team, called the coroner for three bodies, then the EMTs to care for the injured assailant. She asked Robert to take her to the wreck. Robert walked her to the edge. She and Robert both had flashlights. Robert started to descend to show her how to get to the wreck safely. Katrina remained at road level to accept any more emergency vehicles. Lisa approached the overturned pickup and looked inside, confirming everything that Robert described. The survivor had not changed his position. Lisa advised him of his rights and informed him that the paramedics would arrive shortly. She had no intention of moving the man.

Robert stood behind and began interrogating him. Lisa listened, intrigued. "Where is Ali?"

"Abbottabad."

"Who is your contact here?"

The man was hesitant. Lisa understood the situation and broke with protocol, taking her weapon out of her holster. "You tried to kill my friend. I don't think she had any intention to harm you. I, however, would be OK with finishing the job that this man started." To Robert's surprise, she raised the gun and pointed it at the man. "Are we clear about this?"

The man nodded with agreement, suddenly more than ready to divulge details. "He is in Grass Valley, California. He is a doctor. Doctor Terry Sweet."

Robert had heard *that* name before from Katrina as well. *Two common foes in an unholy alliance to eliminate Katrina for revenge.*

Katrina called down to the wreck. "The ambulance is coming up the road!"

Lisa walked back to join Katrina. She directed the ambulance to a spot nearest the injured gunman. She briefed the EMTs on the situation. They retrieved a lightweight litter, rope, and straps and dropped the equipment down to Robert. Then they followed. Once they reached the scene, Robert left and returned to Katrina's side. The EMTs worked on the injured man and checked the driver for vital signs.

As Robert reached the top, a small caravan of vehicles arrived: two coroner trucks and one additional deputy sheriff squad car. Lisa was determined to keep this a local incident. A second deputy sheriff's squad arrived with more people. Uniformed deputies approached Lisa to get an overview and discuss activity. The coroner joined the discussion. Lisa took notes for her soon-to-be lengthy report. Katrina and Robert, exhausted, leaned against the Jeep and watched.

The deputies broke away from Lisa, and some stayed at the scene near the trailer. Before cataloging the evidence, the deputies labeled and photographed everything where it lay. Other deputies went down to the wreck to meet the EMTs as they were transferring the injured man to the litter. The deputies collected more evidence from in and around the vehicle. More photos were taken. The scene of the wreck was a bustle of activity as the coroner arrived to take away the deceased driver.

The sky began to lighten with the approaching dawn. It allowed better visibility for the workers at the crime scene. Above, at the pad, a forensic team continued to investigate the damage to the trailer. The coroner oversaw the process of transferring the three bodies to the van. A deputy collected and packaged the weapons as evidence. The EMT team placed the lone surviving assassin in the ambulance. Lisa called the contracted towing service for a wrecker to lift and haul the truck away. By dawn, the truck had been rolled back onto its wheels and was ready to be pulled up the ravine. The bodies and the coroner's team were gone. Deputies prepared the scene for protection, and the forensic teams completed work to record ballistic damage. Before sealing the trailer, the deputy allowed Katrina and Robert to retrieve anything they needed.

Katrina waited until dawn to place a call to her father and explain what had happened. The trailer was nearly totaled. She asked if she and Robert could land there for a while. Her father said they could—but not indefinitely.

The family was back together, unexpectedly and under dire circumstances. Upon learning who was behind the attacks, Katrina was angry and resolved to retaliate and end the psychic cold war. They had destroyed her home, most of her possessions, and had fully intended to kill her. For the second time in short succession, Robert had saved her. Determined not to be in that vulnerable position ever again, she believed that she had to surrender to the darkness and regress to the role of a sociopath, but she didn't want to do it alone and she needed a plan.

22

... UNSANCTIONED RETALIATION

While seeking revenge at her parents' home, Katrina and Robert continued to grow their lives as a couple. Katrina, Robert, and even Edwin exchanged ideas for a plan to get back at Ali with an appropriate response. As the sheriff's forensic team worked the details on the evidence, Robert and Katrina waited. It took almost a week for them to return to the heavily damaged and shambled hulk. She was anxious about one largely irreplaceable possession—the Hermann Circuit designed and crafted by DD that she had not been able to retrieve the evening of the attack. Katrina was notified by a phone message that her trailer could be transferred back to her possession by meeting with a deputy at the crime scene.

Aside from the lone squad car, law enforcement activity was gone. The trailer was more like a prop from a Hollywood war movie, dotted with bullet holes ripped into the thin corrugated sheet metal. It was a static display of the aftermath of target practice. Glass was shattered or missing in the pocked, cheap, aluminum frame windows. Soiled curtains, some tattered, flailed in the wind. The skirt below remained intact. Curiously, the front door was missing. The deputy met her and Robert on the gravel pad.

They exited the Jeep and slowly gazed upon what was once a peaceful home. Both shuffled toward the steps to the front deck. Katrina went in first. Water had stained and damaged the floor in the kitchen. The refrigerator sustained heavy bullet damage. It was a total loss. The food inside had been left to spoil, causing a foul odor that smelled like a landfill throughout the trailer. Wood cabinets were splintered. Food had spilled or contents exploded from being shot up. Packages and containers were a fragmented mix of cardboard, glass, and metal, spattered with sauces and condiments, evoking a murder scene from a cheap slasher movie. None of the appliances were salvageable. Katrina walked past the demolished TV screen and jagged remains from her modest CD collection, then begrudgingly walked to her bedroom. The mirror over her dresser was decimated and the glass shards scattered on the dresser and carpet. Her closet doors were heavily pockmarked in the middle. She opened what was left of the door, looked up on the shelf above ripped up dresses and jackets—and found her circuit, stowed in a box, unharmed. She brought it down.

As she left the room, glancing at the damage all around, she couldn't help but think that her life had been reduced to pieces, fragments, bits too small to put back together. It brought tears to her eyes. This was her new normal. She realized that no matter how much she changed or grew, she would never be able to eliminate her connection with the past. She would never be able to completely ignore who she was. Her past wouldn't let her.

Robert met her as she entered the living room, once a safe cozy and peaceful room of comfort. He recalled similar scenes of homes destroyed by gunfire. He kept in mind that no one he cared for had been killed here. There was no sign of blood. There were no faces of horror to greet him. Lucky for Katrina, he thought, she would never endure that. For Robert, the carnage that came with the damage would never leave his memory.

Robert went to inspect her clothes. Not all were damaged. Robert's clothes and backpack were under the bed, untouched. His boots in the corner of the room were also unscathed. The bed and mattress were damaged but not beyond repair. Piece by piece, they rummaged through the debris, looking for, and sometimes finding, something that could be salvaged. On this trip, they would take home clothing and essentials.

In subsequent trips, they searched for and inspected anything else they could use: silverware and knives, some pots and pans. Most glasses, dishes, and plates hadn't survived. Katrina found the micaceous clay bowl Mary Ellen had bought for her. It was miraculously intact. She snatched it up and carefully placed it in the Jeep with ample protection. During another visit, they set up a dumpster outside the trailer. They emptied the trailer of all debris, damaged appliances, and furniture. On the final trip, they removed the water-damaged carpeting and began cleaning. Robert then covered the windows, the gaping doorway, and other large holes in the siding with plastic sheeting. The trailer was sealed tight and would remain that way until Robert could begin repairs.

Now, they could focus on a response to the attack. Back in Grass Valley, they met with Edwin at the table to talk. Katrina's father started the discussion.

"You stopped the hired guns, but the leaders have not been stopped. They'll evaluate what happened, make some changes for improvements, and try again, Katrina. They won't make mistakes next time," Edwin explained, sounding very much like a commanding officer.

"I realize that."

"Katrina and I have talked about this a lot. I have to be careful not to let it adversely affect me," said Robert, taking the vial out of his pocket and displaying it for Edwin to see. He opened it and put a drop under his tongue. "We are going to stop them from hurting us again. Katrina's got friends that have helped her before, and she thinks they will help her again."

"We can do it ourselves, Dad," assured Katrina.

Edwin expressed another concern regarding Robert. "Look, I know you were in some sort of Special Forces outfit, and I know why you don't want to talk about it. I respect that. You guys went through hell out there. How do I know you won't snap or do something to jeopardize the plan?"

"Commander, she is all I have. She saved me from myself. I have changed. I have learned how to get back what was taken from me. I have always respected life. In the field, I took so many lives, and I saw so many of my own get killed, I could never allow that to happen to her."

"You killed three men in less than a minute at her trailer."

"Commander, they were there to execute her. They shot up the trailer because she was inside. It was clear they enjoyed doing what they did. It made it easier for me to shoot them."

At that, Edwin left the table. Katrina placed a call to a helper from her past. She called DD for guidance and assistance. DD was pleasantly surprised to get her call after so many years. "I haven't heard from you in almost a decade. Something must be wrong," he said. "Do you need my help?"

"Yes. I was attacked last week, not electromagnetically. Al-Qaeda sent hitmen to kill me with gunfire. They shot up my trailer and most everything inside it."

Katrina told DD about Robert and how Robert had helped her escape, killed three of the terrorists, and received intel from the surviving terrorist that pointed to Ali and Sweet.

DD knew about both men. "Katrina, I can help you with Sweet. He's a vile person. Grudges indicate a weak character and a lack of intelligence. You need to let me eliminate him for good. If he survives, he will come back stronger, and you don't have the resources to defend against what he might try next."

Katrina and DD discussed a plan and possible scenarios. DD indicated he would review the plan then call Katrina the next day to set it in motion.

"But what about Ali?" asked Katrina. He was the more dangerous one. There was a pause as Katrina heard DD breathe deeply as if he regretted what he was about to tell her.

"Ali is a *Company* asset: a *valuable* company asset. He has been helping them keep Al-Qaeda in Pakistan on a leash, in exchange for extending his power in the region. There is no telling what will happen if we lose him. It's a tense situation there with Iraq's stability being threatened."

"He tried to kill me, DD. Are you saying . . . never mind. I know what you are saying. I won't ask you to help me with Ali."

"I am advising you not to do anything unless you want the worst of the CIA to consider you a threat, too."

"How would they know it was me? Would you tell on me?"

There was silence on the other end of the line.

"DD? Would you actually tell on me? I thought you despised sociopaths."

"Katrina! Damn it! They know who you are. They know everything about you. If word leaked about Ali putting a hit on you, they would likely tap your phones. You are considered a 'friendly,' but you are also expendable in comparison to Ali."

Katrina could not accept what she was being told: that her own country placed greater value on a terrorist than herself. And, to make it worse, the man that helped her harness her ability seemed like he was threatening to turn on her.

"I still want to be an ally to you, Katrina. Don't do anything to jeopardize that."

There was no response.

"Katrina? Are you there?"

"Yes."

"Ali is huge to the security of the region. You have no idea how many people have risked their lives, and many did not survive, so we could have someone like him inside." All Katrina could think about was being labeled "expendable."

"Promise me that you will not do anything to Ali that would kill him," DD said.

There was silence again. It lasted longer than DD felt comfortable with. Finally, Katrina relented.

"What happens when he attacks me again, DD? He'll send someone again. Will the *Company* at least give me the courtesy of a warning?"

"Ali has unlimited rights. That's the condition. He could kill someone on 5th Avenue and get away with it. However, the State Department was clever enough to restrict him from entering the country."

"So? How about you? Would you let me know if you found out my life was in danger?"

"I would not let you die at the hands of a terrorist," DD said, and Katrina recognized the sincerity in his voice. He meant it.

"Did you know about the attack?"

"No. I did not, and I probably would not know if there were any plans."

"Well, that's it then. I have to constantly look over my shoulder."

DD failed to offer anything beyond taking care of Sweet. Katrina felt it was time to end the call and move on. It ended awkwardly for both former allies.

As Katrina hung up, Robert took notice of her expression. He let her walk away and sit down, working through her feelings of disgust. She was not in the mood to talk, so he was not going to ask about the call. Then, after a while, she opened up.

"I feel betrayed. I am so.... They said I'm expendable! Ali is like ... untouchable. If I retaliated, first, they would know, then, they would . . ."

She couldn't finish the sentence. Robert sat down next to her and reached out to hold her hand.

Katrina replayed the conversation between her and DD. Robert wasn't surprised. She wasn't the only expendable that he knew. It conjured bitter resentment from his tours as a soldier. Learning that a scoundrel like Ali was granted immunity and protection by the organizations he had defended presented more evidence of how the world had damaged itself through compromised values. He refused to accept it. He refused to feel helpless, and he refused to allow Katrina to feel it, too. Katrina then told him about DD's plan to respond to Sweet's role in the attack. It did not move him.

Neither Katrina nor Robert slept well that night. At this most urgent of times, her only ally besides Robert had abandoned her. Ali would continue to be a powerful threat if he wasn't stopped. She thought about her talks with Mary Ellen and the need to retain a sense of humanity despite the fact her life was in danger. Ali did not deserve the respect and protection to live, only to allow him to destroy again. DD had warned her not to kill.

However, he didn't say anything about giving Ali a scare.

Robert was used to combat, but in his eyes, Katrina was not a combatant. She wasn't exactly the girl next door, and what she carried wasn't any regular type of baggage. She was something unique. Being in her presence gave him a thrill he had not felt since his last tour. To some other guy, this would have been unnerving, affecting the relationship, with all the unknown risks and her crazy ability. But as Katrina was not just another woman, Robert was not just another guy. The recognized risk gave him a feeling of retaining an identity he had proudly possessed as a Ranger in the Iraq and Afghanistan wars.

* * *

Morning came quickly. Edwin was up before everyone else. The RN visited the house shortly afterward to tend to Katrina's mother. Her entrance woke Katrina and Robert up only an hour before DD's call. They rushed out of bed to change and get ready. With little time, they sat at the kitchen table for coffee and waited.

Minutes later, the phone rang. DD was ready to execute the plan regarding Sweet as discussed.

He instructed Katrina to remote view Sweet's office, which she did.

Sweet was at his desk with a reading lamp, buried in reading the morning paper. His computer was on with the screen open to a social media page. Katrina easily read the light energy in the room, redirecting it back to the panel, causing the lamps to emit the telltale flicker. It caught Sweet's attention. He got up from his office chair to check if there was a brownout outside. As he stood up, the lights shut off completely, leaving only his computer screen lit. He stood and witnessed his computer shut down abruptly, darkening the room. The windows, their shades down, allowed only slivers of daylight in. With the darkness came quiet, paralyzing him with fright.

The coward realized his greatest fears, and there was no defense. He lacked the natural ability to fight and used technology to carry out his bullying methods. Now, his equipment wasn't ready for a psychokinetic attack. Taking his keys, he rushed to the door, looking to exit the building.

DD sensed everything that was happening. His protégé was measured, precise, and demonstrated good timing. Now it was his time to act. Katrina didn't know precisely what he had in mind and preferred not to dwell on it. DD communicated to Sweet, telepathically, as Sweet stumbled out of the building, and ran for his car.

"Sweet, you pitiful fool, you are going to die! The Company *will be pleased by this, finally rid of your insolence and conceit. You are a loose cannon. You have been careless and you have abused your position too many times. Attacking Katrina with hitmen went beyond what I thought you were capable of. You overstepped your utility."*

Sweet got into his car and drove off quickly. DD read into his mind. Sweet was driving at a high rate of speed, heading for his lab at the university. DD focused on Sweet. He sensed Sweet's heart rate increase.

Goodbye, Doctor Sweet.

DD pulsed energy directly to the heart, causing a cardiac arrest. Sweet lost consciousness and the car veered off the road, slamming into a light pole. Katrina sensed everything. She remained silent as DD assassinated the rogue scientist.

"He's dead," she observed, as unemotionally as her conscience could allow.

Robert looked at her, realizing she had taken part in the kill. She did not want DD to read her mind as she realized her work was not done.

"Katrina, understand that I did not kill Sweet for you," DD said when they spoke again. "I did it because the *Company* recognized he had overstepped his authority. That resulted in his death. Ali will eventually learn that Sweet was killed. We will make sure of that. We will plant guilt on him by convincing him that he was partially responsible for Sweet's death. That may be enough to cause him to think twice before trying to kill you again."

Katrina offered no response to indicate her concurrence.

DD emphasized his points. "I know what you are planning to do. I am advising you, and I am going to be stern, be careful. I will not help you. You are on your own from now on. If you make a mistake in your attack and kill him, you will be hunted down. We have many like Ali in other countries and continents. Some are more diabolical than he is, dealing in drugs, arms, and child prostitution. If they learn that we cannot protect Ali, they will question our ability to protect them. It will damage our national security."

Katrina remained silent, taking in DD's long, detailed warning.

"Katrina, I strongly recommend you reconsider your response."

Finally, she spoke. "He is a threat, DD. He will always be a threat. Appeasement has never been a successful response to the acts of narcissists. He is not going to let it go."

"If you kill him, you will have a short future. If you injure him, and he survives, he will come back at you, hard. Are you sure you want that?" DD asked.

"Then I will always be looking over my shoulder, regardless of what I do."

"In this line of business, there is no normal life, and everyone eventually has a price on their head. Also, there are no permanent allies, and the breakup could be extreme."

Katrina heard the message loud and clear. "So, we're breaking up? This call is our last DD?"

"We may see each other again under different conditions. I bear no malice toward you, and I know you mean the same toward me."

The call ended, pale, sterile. Two simple generic goodbyes that better resembled a telemarketer's call than two people who had partnered through multiple murders and heroics. Katrina hung up hurt, beyond disappointed. She was going to show Ali how much of a force she could be.

Thirteen hours ahead, in Abbottabad, Ali was getting ready to leave his office laboratory. Ali was considered immune to prosecution by the United States because of his status as a valuable informant on Islamic extremist activity. In reality, Ali was feeding the CIA useless information about actors who were not considered within the circle of influence in Al-Qaeda.

Ali continued to work on psychokinetic research. His project was still behind where he wanted to be. Funding used to be better when he was able to use the drug cartels to support the work. That was until a joint US–Pakistani effort made things perilous and difficult. There were forces that fought to keep the poppy competition in Afghanistan more dominant. Ali worked to be more active in oil in Qatar, but even there, trust was hard to gain, and his financial power was not enough to get what he needed to keep his operation going fluently. Consequently, he obtained loans fraudulently through Deutsche Bank, and he was highly in debt.

He was stressed, tired, and ready to leave for the day when a loud explosion shook his windowless building, causing complete darkness for a moment until the backup generators activated. It reminded him of ... Katrina. His team had failed. He had not asked for the details.

He decided to call Sweet. There was no answer. Still in the lab, with a few other researchers and operators, he went back to his desk to send a message to Sweet. As he pressed the send button, there was another loud pop outside the building, and the lights and computers went out again. People in the lab reached for flashlights. Someone mentioned that the generator backfired and failed.

Ali was officially concerned. He used his own ability to try to locate Katrina. He couldn't find her. Katrina was using the Hermann Circuit. Then Katrina broke contact.

The cramped lab was almost impassable with workers aimlessly grazing by their workstations, blocking access to the exit. His people recognized the horror in his face. Finally reaching the exit, he could hear emergency vehicles approach. The telltale smell of the smoke from the burning transformer lingered.

Ali escaped without physical harm. Katrina's pinpoint accuracy made him aware that she could have killed him if she had really wanted to. Not wanting to let others win battles, he put this episode away for another time when he would be better equipped and informed to deal with Katrina ... for the last time.

23

. . . CLOSURE

Emma and Katrina had been talking for hours when the rising sun colored the sky a dark shade of pink. They both gazed out the window in appreciation of another day on Earth. The workday was about to begin, but not for them.

Katrina resumed her story. "Bob and I stayed with Grandma and Grandpa until Bob was able to fix the trailer. It took a long time, but we did it. As you know, we stayed there for a few years after he fixed it, to build up some money to afford what we have now. When Bob got the job as a security consultant, and I became an engineer in Taos, things really got better."

"Bob turned out to be a great carpenter, didn't he?" Emma asked. "If it hadn't been for him, you would have lost everything. Knowing his background and everything he went through, I'm now more impressed with him than I was before. It's interesting to think that you two would not have met if you hadn't helped me move into the dorm that day. And if you hadn't met him, who knows what would have happened to you in that trailer? Or what would have happened to him? Because of you, he learned to manage his PTSD and got sober fast. Amazing."

"It is remarkable. We don't realize the impact each of us may have on others until long after the act. That's why I think the true meaning of life is simply to make life better for others."

Emma paused, looking at her mother intently. "I didn't know anything about your ability, and you kept that part of your life so private from me. I don't remember the embassy. I remember seeing ice cubes in the tub. I remember the sonic boom at Grandma's house. I think I had thought it was a plane that flew too fast and low. What about the scientists that harassed you? Are they still alive? Aren't you concerned they might attack you again some time?"

Katrina thought of not replying, but her daughter deserved full, honest answers after being subjected to her mother's secrecy for so long, in the name of her protection. "Bob and I get harassed once in a while but not through electromagnetic energy. They spy on us. I still have a lukewarm relationship with DD. The scientists know that, and DD even made it clear to them I am off-limits. DD is practically retired. Doctor Loom doesn't want to deal with DD anymore. I think we'll be OK as long we keep our guard up. Bob has made contact with some guys in intelligence and Special Forces through his consultations. They have our backs."

"What about Sonny Lyle, the Chi instructor?"

"I never heard from him again after he introduced me to DD."

"There are so many others you mentioned. Have you had contact with Lauren, the remote viewing scientist?" Emma asked, as if running down a checklist.

"Dr. Lauren Beauchard has written a number of books on the psychic phenomenon. I see her at UFO conferences. We communicate through social media."

"What happened to Ali and Elahi?"

"Ali taunts me with email. He is a jealous, immature man. He is still banned from the United States. Bob sought help from men that he worked with in the State Department, and they update him on Ali and his whereabouts. They told him that any connections Ali had with cells in the United States don't exist anymore. That doesn't mean he is completely out of the picture."

"And Elahi?" Emma pressed.

"Elahi is a changed man. He still lives in Switzerland, working with his son at CERN. His son turned him around. He is no longer involved in human trafficking and went to therapy for anger management. Elahi found me a few years ago and sent me a letter of apology. Appearing at psychic and UFO conferences makes me highly visible. Even though I am not a presenter, word gets around ...oh, Elahi is even a happy grandfather."

Emma chuckled. "You never know, do you?"

"That change surprised me, I admit," Katrina replied.

"Are you still friends with Mary Ellen?"

"Absolutely! We are the best of friends. I have visited her at Dulce for Little Beaver Days quite a few times now. She told me she is planning to visit Robert and me soon. I am looking forward to that. Now, I think I need to get some sleep before I fly home. How about you?"

"Yeah, me too."

"You should come and visit Bob and me in Taos. I'm sure Bob would be more open with you after I tell him about our talk. Plus, you are my only child, and I have always loved you and protected you. I really am proud of the woman you became. Just stay away from Grass Valley."

Emma smiled and moved close to hug Katrina. Katrina returned the hug, a happy face with eyes closed, taking in the embrace. Before they left for the airport, Katrina wrote Emma another short note. Emma found it on the kitchen counter upon her return.

> *There are times when I think about the different hardships I have had throughout and have wondered how I did not go crazy or lose my life. My initial purpose was to serve, to heal, to protect, to bring out the best, and how I got hit so hard by darker forces and evil people made me at times wonder ... but it is the kindnesses that we bestow on one another that rekindles the heart, spirit, mind, and renews a faith like no other.*

THE END

ACKNOWLEDGMENTS

This book would not have been written without the continued support from my wife, Janice.

The story is a fictionalized version of real events. The characters are based on real people.

The main character is portrayed as a strong, resilient, ethical, and sincere woman. She mirrors the real person Katrina is based on.

Leslie K. Wilkins-Hillerman opened up to me and let me in on her deepest feelings regarding the many challenges encountered in her life.

Leslie confided to me that engaging with me while I wrote this story was cathartic and liberating. I am honored that she trusted me with her most personal stories and allowed me the freedom to piece together episodes into a coherent, informative yarn, giving readers both insight and thrills.

I am grateful for her continued friendship for so many years.

ABOUT THE AUTHOR

Paul G. Vecchiet is the author of *The Disclosure Paradox*, a science-fiction series that explores the ethical, psychological, and institutional consequences of anomalous human capability.

Drawing on a background in government service, management, and long-standing interest in suppressed science and human consciousness, Vecchiet's work examines how extraordinary phenomena are handled when they intersect with secrecy, power, and fear. His stories focus less on spectacle than on consequence—particularly the human cost of exploitation by institutions unequipped to confront what they do not fully understand.

Rather than offering conclusions, Vecchiet's novels present speculative frameworks that invite inquiry into the limits of science, the burden of knowledge, and the moral responsibility that accompanies discovery.

He lives in West Virginia and continues to write fiction that challenges certainty while remaining grounded in character, discipline, and restraint.

www.ingramcontent.com/pod-product-compliance
Lightning Source LLC
LaVergne TN
LVHW040058080526
838202LV00045B/3688